WITHDRAWN

# THE PRINCESSES OF ATLANTIS

Also by Lisa Williams Kline

*Eleanor Hill*

# THE Princesses
# of ATLANTIS

## LISA WILLIAMS KLINE

Cricket Books
Chicago

Copyright © 2002 by Lisa Williams Kline
All rights reserved
Printed in the United States of America
Designed by Ron McCutchan
First edition, 2002

Library of Congress Cataloging-in-Publication Data

Kline, Lisa Williams.
  The princesses of Atlantis / Lisa Williams Kline.—1st ed.
     p. cm.
Summary: Twelve-year-old best friends Carly and Arlene write about
twin princesses during the final, cataclysmic days of Atlantis in a story
that parallels the growing tensions the two friends are experiencing
in their lives.
  ISBN 0-8126-2855-1 (cloth : alk. paper)
  [1. Best friends—Fiction. 2. Friendship—Fiction. 3. Identity—Fiction.
4. Schools—Fiction. 5. Authorship—Fiction. 6. Atlantis—Fiction.]
I. Title.
  PZ7.K67935 Pr 2002
  [Fic]—dc21

                                                      2002000590

For the family of my childhood
—Mom, Dad, and Pat—

the family of my adulthood
—Jeff, Caitlin, and Kelsey—

and the writers in my life who are my family, too

# chapter 1

## *Arlene and Me*

ARLENE LIES CROSSWAYS ON her bed with her long, bony legs propped against the wall. She takes off her glasses, which are slightly steamed from the heat, uses the end of her T-shirt to clean them, then puts them back on. Seventh grade starts next week, and we're in what they call the dog days of August. I always thought that meant people are so hot they lie around panting, but Arlene has informed me that it actually has something to do with the stars.

"O.K., Carly, read what we've got so far," she says.

"'Ten thousand years ago when the earth was tender and people still believed in magic, there was an island kingdom called Atlantis. And in that kingdom lived identical twin princesses named . . . blank and blank,'" I read. Arlene always sprawls on the bed and thinks things up while I sit at the desk and type. We're writing a novel together about the kingdom of Atlantis, an ancient civilization of great riches that mysteriously fell into the sea and disappeared, never to be found again. "So, what should we name our princesses?" I say.

"How about Eva for one of them?"

"Princess Eva?" I try out the sound of it.

"Sure," says Arlene. "Like in the Garden of Eden."

I shove my hair behind my ears and adjust my glasses. Arlene and I have been friends since second grade. Arlene is tall for a twelve-year-old, thin and knock-kneed. She wears glasses, and her ears stick out. I'm the shortest in my class, "pleasingly plump," as my grandmother so embarrassingly calls it—and coincidentally, I also have glasses and ears that stick out.

1

"And her twin sister's name could be Lydia." From the tone of Arlene's voice, I can tell that she's already made up her mind.

"Princess Eva and Princess Lydia." I picture two sleek-haired Atlantean princesses whose smooth, tawny skin contrasts with their flowing golden tunics. Their ears definitely do not stick out.

Arlene's room is on the third floor of her family's old Victorian house. It has a sloped ceiling and a tiny dormer window with a wooden window seat. Her mother let her paint the room any way she wanted, so she picked light blue walls with clouds and a navy-blue ceiling with stars.

This room is where we create our literary masterpieces. With the stars and all, I feel like I'm just about in heaven. One day in third grade, we discovered that the floor is slanted. We had gone up to Arlene's room with our skates on (which you are not allowed to do at my house) and found that if you stand beside the door, you automatically roll toward the window. At that time we believed the slope of the floor might be enough for a running start to push off and fly right out.

Arlene rolls over onto her stomach, then to her back. In an exercise I've seen my mom do, she opens and closes her legs a few times. Arlene has an old-fashioned, white chenille bedspread with lots of little nubs on it that make a pattern like a big star, and she has the imprints of the nubs on the backs of her legs.

What I love about Arlene is her brain. It goes everywhere, anywhere, and comes back with a story. When I'm with Arlene, I'm no longer quiet, mousy Carly. I can be anybody. I can be Lucy from *The Lion, the Witch and the Wardrobe* or Huck Finn from *The Adventures of Tom Sawyer.* In second grade, while the other kids played soccer or Barbies after school, Arlene and I cut the fingers out of outgrown winter gloves and played Oliver Twist learning how to pick pockets. I was Oliver to Arlene's Dodger. When we played *The Sword in the Stone,* Arlene was Merlyn and I was the Wart.

st year in sixth grade, the kids started to make fun of her
ng, skinny legs and the way she walks down the hall at
hool waving her thin arms while she talks. Once while
lling me something, she accidentally smacked Jeremy Glea-
n right in the face. Sometimes they laughed at me, too. Even
ough it doesn't bother me all that much, I'm hoping that
is year they won't laugh. So far Arlene hasn't noticed.
metimes I think as good friends we should talk about it, but
her times I'm sure that truly good friends would never
ention it at all.

.K." I READ OUR first paragraph again to see how it sounds
th the new names. "'Ten thousand years ago when the
rth was tender and people still believed in magic, there was
island kingdom called Atlantis. And in that kingdom lived
ntical twin princesses named Eva and Lydia.'" And now
incesses Eva and Lydia exist. I'm already deciding which of
m will be me.

Arlene's father, who teaches English literature, says the
t person to tell the story of Atlantis was the famous Greek
cher named Plato, and that Atlantis is one of the great mys-
ies of civilization. Arlene and I like that. Plato said the
ople of Atlantis were strong, smart, and beautiful and loved
 sea. But they became so power hungry and greedy that
seidon, the god of the sea, punished them by causing an
thquake, a volcanic explosion, and a tidal wave that sank
antis to the bottom of the ocean in one day.

Mom, on the other hand, says most real scholars don't
nk Atlantis ever existed. She said people have written
oks by the dozens, trying to prove Atlantis was in the
ddle of the Atlantic Ocean, off the coast of the Bahamas,
mewhere near Turkey, off the coast of Greece, or even in
tarctica. No one has ever found it. She gave us some
oks, just to prove it. She says Plato made Atlantis up.

Arlene and I believe in Atlantis. Just because no one has

We never fought about who wanted to play who[ example, when we played *The Little Mermaid,* I wanted to be the little mermaid, and Arlene didn't, b she said the little mermaid was doomed. "She's a m and she wants to be a person," she explained. "In lit characters who want to be something they're not ar trouble. I'll be the sea witch."

Now that we're in middle school, we do more g stuff, such as recite entire scenes from *Little Women* and *Sensibility.* In *Little Women* I am always Amy, an is always Jo. In *Sense and Sensibility* Arlene is alwa and I am always Marianne.

Arlene's family moved to North Carolina from M setts when her father took a teaching job at the col mother is a music teacher. Two weeks after they m the creaky old Victorian on Wendover Street, they hi lege student who painted the outside purple. T books piled everywhere at Arlene's, and there's alwa playing. They have two golden retrievers, and her ho cozily like dogs. Her parents listen to classical music Carly Simon-type stuff on the first floor, and on th floor Arlene's older sister, Juliet, sings to rap and in her underwear, using an empty toilet roll for phone. Arlene and I think this is really dumb.

I've lived in North Carolina all my life. My dac doctor, and my mom teaches biology at the coll have an annoying younger brother named Matt. W sensible brick house, have a family dinner three tim and strive for five fruits and vegetables a day. Mo middle of trying to win a grant for a research pro something to do with the brain development of t she's going up to the lab all the time.

At my house, flying's not an option since my the first floor. No one in my house is crazy, and I wish I lived at Arlene's.

There is one little thing about Arlene I think of

found it yet doesn't mean they won't someday. Arlene says we should definitely write about the volcano, earthquake, and tidal wave, because that would be a good action scene in case they make a movie out of our book. And I am wondering if Eva and Lydia will survive. Maybe only one princess will survive. I wonder which one it will be.

Arlene is best at descriptions, so she writes those, and I'm best at dialogue, so I write that. We've finished chapter one, and I have just hit Print when we hear Arlene's dad get home.

"I have rediscovered Jane!" He shouts it so loud we can hear him on the third floor. Arlene runs down to the stair landing. I follow her. Her sister, Juliet, who is popular and pretty and everything that Arlene and I are not, is already there. She rolls her eyes at us.

"Jane who?" I whisper.

"Jane Austen," Juliet tells me. "Dad rediscovers her every summer when he's getting his lectures ready." Dr. Welch has long arms, which he waves around a lot like Arlene. Whenever he's home, you think everyone is in a play or something. He is tall and pale, with a halfhearted beard and wire-rim glasses. The two golden dogs run to greet him, weaving in excited circles around his knees.

"What a wit, that Jane!" he shouts. "What an absolute delight!"

We watch from above as Arlene's mother passes him in the hallway. "Oh, how very splendid, darling," she says with a fake English accent. The two dogs follow her into the music room, their plumy tails switching like metronomes. Arlene's mom has brown, shiny hair like Juliet's, which she pulls back into a bun at the nape of her long neck. She has long, graceful arms and fingers and plays piano, harp, and violin. Juliet takes after her, and Arlene takes after Dr. Welch.

Arlene decides this is a great time to act out one of the many scenes she and I have memorized from *Sense and Sensibility*, which of course was written by none other than that very witty Jane Austen. (Not that we have actually *read* Jane Austen. The print is extremely small, and the sentences extremely long. But we've watched all the movies.)

I can act out scenes just fine when it's Arlene and me, but an audience gives me terrible stage fright. So terrible I'm completely paralyzed except for my heart, which pumps so hard the blood roars through my head with a sound like a runaway train. I feel like fainting and throwing up at the same time.

But Arlene loves an audience. She is dazzling, she exudes energy, she grows bigger than life. So now she steps forward, laying on the English accent. "Marianne, you must know by now that Willoughby was acting a part, deceiving you, pretending to be someone he was not."

I'm supposed to say, "Elinor, you are quite wrong. I know he had feelings for me . . . once." Pretty simple, right? But four pairs of eyes are focused on me, and Arlene's entire family is waiting for me to be just as witty as they are, not to mention have just as good a fake English accent. Instantly my cheeks go hot as a summer sidewalk, and nothing will come out of my throat but a giggle. Black spots crowd my vision, blood roars in my head, and saliva rushes to my mouth. I cannot even move. Long, miserable seconds drag by.

At last Arlene jumps in front of me and says my line, then leaps two feet away and says her next line, which is "Dearest sister, I beg you, try to forget him," and jumps back in front of me with "Very well, Elinor. For your sake, I shall try." Her English accent is so exaggerated, she sounds like she has marbles in her mouth. Arlene's whole family applauds, especially her dad. Playing two parts at once is a piece of cake for Arlene. She bows deeply, and I am jealous, because she is just floating on the warm waves of all that applause.

# chapter 2

## *Atlantis*

TEN THOUSAND YEARS AGO when the earth was tender and people still believed in magic, there was an island kingdom called Atlantis. And in that kingdom lived identical twin princesses named Eva and Lydia.

Their father, King Avalach, was fabulously wealthy. Eva and Lydia had multicolored tunics with gold threads for every day of the year. They had gold and silver earrings, ankle bracelets, and necklaces that sang like wind chimes when they moved. They had sailboats with silken sails in all colors of the rainbow, woven from the royal silkworms, and a stable of sleek racehorses with arched necks and nervous, dancing feet. The king had given them hand-carved bows with gold-and-jeweled inlays and ruby-tipped arrows for protection against saber-toothed tigers, mastodons, and sea monsters.

Every night before they went to sleep, Eva and Lydia sat with crossed legs, facing each other among the silken pillows on their enormous canopy bed. By the light of the moon and stars, they touched fingertips and chanted a rhyme they had made up when they were small:

> *Always together,*
> *never apart.*
> *Your thoughts are my thoughts . . .*
> *your heart is my heart.*

Eva and Lydia had a habit of finishing each other's sentences and, on rainy days, played games where they tried to read each other's mind. They practiced mind reading a lot, because Atlantis happened to be having a lot of rain. Sometimes the people of Atlantis enjoyed a clear, sunny morning, but by afternoon high winds, thunder, lightning, and rain came down, first in big, sloppy drops and then in loud, pounding sheets. Every week there were mud slides and flash floods. Ominous puffs of smoke leaked from the dormant volcano west of the city. There had even been a few minor earthquakes. Some of the poorer people of Atlantis lost their homes and had to move to higher ground. King Avalach and Queen Lannu were convinced the gods were very angry indeed and stayed up late, night after night, discussing what might be done. Meanwhile, the palace had become quite muddy. Lacy green mold grew on the lovely imported tile. No one's tunics ever seemed to get completely dry.

Lydia and Eva had never really succeeded at mind reading, in spite of their diligent practice. If Lydia tried to send Eva the message "I'm so mad at Mom and Dad for not letting us learn astronomy like the boys," Eva would just see the color red. And when Eva tried to send Lydia a message, such as "Kick Atlan (their brother) under the table," Lydia might receive a message that seemed to be "Trick lap stand in the stable," which of course made no sense.

It was a custom for royal children in Atlantis, when they turned thirteen, to have parties and receive lavish gifts every day for a whole month, and to get tattooed on the left shoulder with an animal figure of their choice. This tattoo was to symbolize the journey from childhood to adulthood. Eva wanted a mastodon. Lydia was leaning toward a butterfly, but Eva was trying to convince her to get a mastodon, too. At the age of thirteen, the princesses of Atlantis were also supposed to have their husbands chosen for them.

In the month before Eva and Lydia's thirteenth birthday,

the king and queen should have been planning for all of this, but the truth was they were so worried about the rain that they forgot. Eva and Lydia didn't really mind not having the parties. They didn't even mind not having the gifts, and they were quite happy not to have husbands. They did want tattoos, however. One morning they decided to march into the royal throne room and ask for them.

They tiptoed down the white marble walkway to their parents' thrones. The path was lined with golden statues of past kings and queens of Atlantis. The soaring roof above their heads was made of ivory studded with gold and silver, and the pillars reflected the soft pinkish glow of orichalcum, or mountain copper, nearly as valuable as gold. The walls were covered with beautiful frescoes depicting the kings and queens of Atlantis as well as various animals, such as antelopes, mastodons, monkeys, and saber-toothed cats. No one was there.

"Mother? Father?" Eva called softly. Eva was a tawny girl with wild, kinky hair, almond-shaped eyes, and tiny, exquisite ears. "You're sure you don't want a mastodon tattoo?" she whispered to her sister. "What about a baby one, with a cute little furry head?"

"Well, O.K." Eva could talk Lydia into practically anything. Unlike Eva, Lydia wore her hair braided, mostly because Eva liked braiding it. "It's spooky in here," she whispered.

The twins tried sitting on their parents' enormous thrones, dangling their small, sandaled feet. They changed places and pretended to be issuing orders. Suddenly their parents swept into the hall followed by a number of nervous attendants and officials. Eva grabbed Lydia's hand and pulled her under the stone table between the thrones where the crowns and scepters were kept. The girls sat very silent and still.

Their father, King Avalach, was a big man, with shoulders made massive from riding mastodons and hauling sails at sea. He had an ugly scar on his cheek that people said had been inflicted by one of his brothers, and a diadem made from the skin of a male sea ram to show he was descended from Poseidon. Their mother, Queen Lannu, wore a floor-length white tunic, and her long, black hair spilled from a wide, jeweled headband made from the snowy skin of a female sea ram.

King Avalach was in a very bad mood. As he strode down the long hall, he repeatedly slapped his thigh with the ceremonial ankus carried by all soldiers who had victoriously ridden a mastodon into battle.

"As you asked, Your Highness," said Rixor, the head scribe, bowing deeply, "I have summoned the wise men of Atlantis for their advice about the weather."

King Avalach pounded the tabletop right over Eva's and Lydia's heads. "Well, somebody better have some ideas! Pretty soon we'll be rowing boats down the streets!" He wrung several drops of water from his blond beard as he spoke.

"Try to calm down, dear," suggested Queen Lannu.

The head scribe introduced the wise men one by one, and they bowed. There was the priest, who wore a tall headdress of peacock feathers and a flowing red tunic. There was the mathematician, who wore a skullcap and a black tunic with wide sleeves. And there was the engineer, dressed in rough, brown work clothes.

Queen Lannu arched her thin eyebrows. "Weren't there originally four wise men?" Her husband and the other men began to laugh.

"Well, yes, my dear, there was Da, the astronomer," said King Avalach, still amused. "But a year ago he predicted a severe drought." The wise men laughed even harder. "We haven't asked *his* opinion much lately."

The wise men then spoke. The mathematician said the equations all pointed to a sunny future. The engineer said the rain would soon stop of its own accord, and there was no reason to delay the construction of the new sports stadium. The priest claimed to have gotten his information from the rain god, Driz, himself.

"I suggest," he said, his peacock-feather headdress swaying as he spoke, "that His Majesty offer his two daughters as brides for the rain god, Driz."

"Brides for the rain god?" Queen Lannu repeated.

"The girls are exceedingly charming and graceful," said the priest. "I predict Driz would be satisfied, and the rain would stop."

Hidden under the table, Eva and Lydia stared at each other in horror.

# chapter 3

## Frog Eggs

MOM AND I ARE in the girls' department at a store in the mall. The hangers squeal as all the mothers and daughters slide the clothes along the racks. This, I think, is the perfect chance to find a new, exotic me. Sometimes I pretend that I'm secretly descended from mermaid royalty and that my family isn't my real family at all. But it's hard to focus on my daydream because Mom is talking about all the extracurricular activities she wants me to participate in once school starts.

"What about the newspaper staff, Carly? You'd be great at that." Mom holds out an old-fashioned box-shaped dress. "What about this?"

"I don't like it."

"Or the group that does the video news in the morning. That seems like fun, and it would be excellent experience." She holds out a boring white button-up sweater. "This looks useful."

"Not to me."

"Well, what about the yearbook staff? Or the Young Scientists Club?" she says brightly. "I would have loved to join a group like that when I was young. Girls can't get too much science on their transcripts." Mom holds out a shapeless pair of pants. "These?"

"NO!"

I go into the dressing room, put on the cool, skimpy tops and the tight, shiny hiphuggers they wear in the ads, and look in the mirror. It's still plain old me. Pleasingly plump with limp hair and thick glasses and ears that stick out. I'm too big for the girls' sizes and too small for the juniors. Somewhere hatefully in between.

"You're the perfect size for a twelve-year-old," says Mom patiently when I point this out.

Right. I look like Mr. Potato Head. A potato with two little lumpy eyes at the top and toothpicks sticking out instead of arms and legs. And don't forget my radar ears.

Since Arlene's ears stick out, too, she and I have experimented with a few ways to flatten them. One night we wore tight, stretchy headbands to bed. Another night we taped our ears back with masking tape, which pulled some of our hair out by the roots when we took it off. It hurt like crazy. We even tried rubber cement, which left us threading little rubbery balls out of our hair for a week. We always told each other at school the next day that our ears looked much better. But they didn't, and we knew it.

Mom is thin, and her ears do not stick out. She hands in some "appropriate" clothes that she knows fit the middle-school dress code. I pull on the cotton T-shirts and baggy khakis, and guess what. I still look exactly like Mr. Potato Head. With my body, I am never going to look cool.

When Mom asks me how I'm doing a few minutes later, I tell her I don't like anything and I want to go home. When this shopping trip started, I was tingling with excitement. In less than an hour, I've plunged to complete despair.

She comes in, sees my expression, and sits on the little dressing room seat. "Carly, you look darling in those things."

"I don't want to look 'darling.'" I yank the clothes off and throw them on the seat beside Mom.

"Well, then, let's go look for something else."

"No. I'll wear my clothes from last year."

"You've outgrown them."

"I don't want anything." I clamp my hands over my ears and close my eyes.

Mom sighs and looks at her watch. "I have to get to the

lab, Carly. Please, let's just get these so you'll at least have something." She picks up the clothes I threw on the seat and starts folding them.

"I'm not wearing them!" I yell after her as she marches out of the dressing room. "They'll hang in my closet and rot!"

Mom buys the clothes, anyway. She and I don't speak until she pulls into her usual parking space next to the biology building.

"This won't take long," Mom says when I groan. "I've just got to give two frogs injections so they'll make eggs tomorrow. Come on." She jumps out and takes the steps two at a time.

Dappled shadows from dogwood trees dance across the word BIOLOGY engraved on a white stone lintel above the door. I follow her past Eldon, the biology building mascot, a skeleton sitting with his legs crossed in a classroom chair in the front hall. He wears a different outfit for every season of the year and major holidays. During spring break he wore a snorkel and fins. He wore boxers with hearts on them for Valentine's Day. Today, since it's still summer, he's wearing California jams, a sun visor, and flip-flops. Students move him when they walk by, so he's never in the same position.

I follow Mom down the cool halls with the startlingly shiny linoleum floors. Mom's pace is brisk, energetic. At home her thoughts often seem to be somewhere else. That somewhere else, I've learned, is here.

We go down to the basement, where the frogs are kept in plastic containers. It's cold there, and the floor is hard concrete with a drain in the center. Mom pulls out a container where two fat, greenish yellow females float, their small eyes just beneath the water. Male frogs are kept in a separate container marked Boys. She puts on rubber gloves, then draws hormone solution into a hypodermic needle and flicks it to get rid of the air bubble. When she reaches into the bin, both frogs swim frantically to escape, and when she catches one, it struggles, splashing water everywhere. Mom grips it around the middle and swiftly sinks the hypodermic into its lightly speckled thigh. In just a few seconds she has repeated the process with the other frog. She slides the bin back on the shelf with the others and inserts a green, laminated color code into the front label to show that these frogs will be ready to produce eggs in the morning.

"I'm built exactly like a frog," I say now.

"You are not." She waves me out of the room and swings the heavy door shut.

"Am so."

"Carly, I know you're upset about your body," she says as we head back upstairs. "But you're at an awkward age. And I promise you it's only temporary."

"I bet you were never built like a frog. Or Mr. Potato Head."

Mom strides down the hall past Eldon at such a pace I have to trot to keep up with her. I can tell I've made her mad again. She looks impatient when she holds the front door open for me, but I still feel like complaining.

"And I bet your mom never made you buy clothes that you didn't even like." I get in the van and slam the door.

She slams her door. Uh-oh. I've gone too far. "My mom *made* my clothes," she says, "because we didn't have the money to buy them!" We don't speak the rest of the way home. When we get inside the house, she shoves the department store bag into my arms. It rattles angrily. "Take that to your room," she says.

I put on the baggiest shirt I own. Then I call Arlene and ask her if she wants to work on our novel. She says yes, and I stomp by Mom, who glares at me from behind the kitchen counter. I get on my bike and ride over to Arlene's. As I pedal across the campus quad, the white-columned brick buildings shimmer in the heat. They seem to have been there since the dawn of time. I ride past the biology building and look up at Mom's office window. It's shaped like a half-moon, and she has hanging baskets of spider plants with lots of babies. The window looks like a big eye with fluffy eyelashes, watching me.

I leave the college and ride past the swimming pool where most of the kids in the neighborhood hang out in the summer, including my brother, Matt, and Arlene's sister, Juliet. The sun turns the water a dazzling whitish green, and I can almost smell the chlorine. Juliet is in a clump of tanned girls and boys at the edge of the pool. They are jostling around, laughing and trying to push each other in. The lifeguard stops twirling her whistle just long enough to blow it and yell at them. Matt is bouncing on the high board. I'd recognize that wiry body and green, zinc oxide nose anywhere. As I ride by, he does a perfect one and a half. Not bad for a third grader. I envy Matt. He never stops moving. He plays soccer, basketball, and softball during the school year and swims all summer. He does his homework standing up, and even his spelling lists have this smudged racing slant to them. He does not take or even need time to sit around and *think*.

In less than half an hour, I'm up in Arlene's bedroom typing, and I am Princess Lydia, who has a different tunic for every day of the year and looks nothing like Mr. Potato Head. After a few minutes Arlene and I take a break to talk about the concept of "pretty." Arlene does the scissors exercise with her long, skinny legs again. Her mom is washing the bedspread because we accidentally spilled chocolate milk on it, so she's just lying on her sheets, which I notice don't match. Sheets in my house always match. At my house we're not even allowed to drink chocolate milk in our bedrooms. Downstairs a piano student of Mrs. Welch's, who obviously didn't practice much last week, is stumbling through what Arlene has told me is a Beethoven sonatina.

"I tried on clothes today," I tell her. "I looked terrible in everything. Mom made me buy all these clothes that look totally horrendous on me." I start to mention my breast buds that look like Mr. Potato Head eyes, but decide not to, since last time we showered at the pool, I noticed Arlene didn't have any.

"Carly, nobody in literature is *pretty*." Arlene tries a yoga pose that resembles a pretzel.

"What do you mean?" I say.

"Jo March wasn't pretty. Meg in *A Wrinkle in Time* was big and awkward, and in chapter one she even got a bruise on her hip."

"You're right!" I clap my hands to my head. "Mary Lennox in *The Secret Garden* was one of the most unpleasant-looking children anyone had ever seen."

Arlene untangles herself from the yoga pose, gets up from the bed, and rifles through her bookshelf. She holds out *Charlotte's Web*. "Charlotte was a true friend and a good writer, but pretty? I don't think so. Not with eight hairy legs." She replaces the book on the shelf, throws her arms in the air as if to say "case closed," and collapses on the bed. "I personally would be embarrassed to be *pretty*. It lacks character."

"Absolutely," I say with conviction. "Where were we? Oh yeah, Lydia and Eva, who are not pretty but who have tons of character, find out they're supposed to marry the rain god, Driz." At this point I don't want to admit to Arlene that I had indeed imagined Lydia and Eva to be pretty, in fact to be beautiful. If I tell her, she might think I'm shallow.

"Right, they're not pretty. But they have charisma. People are drawn to them, drawn to their inner beauty."

"Inner beauty?" I wonder if Arlene is secretly picturing them to be pretty, too.

"Yeah, inner beauty."

We write all afternoon. Arlene acts out the parts, and I type. Mrs. Welch's student finally goes home. Arlene's father arrives, and Juliet gets back from the pool. We hear her telling her mom how Craig Weisener's bathing suit came off after he did a one and a half and how funny he was trying to pull it back up underwater. She talks about his cute buns, which embarrasses Arlene and me. Arlene's father tells her that this is not among the qualities she should look for in a young man, and she tells him Craig is too young for her, anyway. Juliet comes upstairs, and the floor of Arlene's room starts to vibrate as loud music seeps through.

"We can't concentrate!" Arlene bangs her foot on the floor.

The phone rings. We don't bother to answer it, because Juliet has perfected Olympic phone answering and can grab it before the end of the first ring.

"Carly!" shouts Juliet. "You have to go home for dinner."

I groan. "Can I eat here?"

Arlene runs out on the landing. "Mom," she shouts, "can Carly stay for dinner?"

"Carly, your mother says she heard that, and no, you can't," Juliet shouts.

"A little less noise there," intones Arlene's father from his study down below, just like Wendy's father in *Peter Pan*.

I get on my bike. In slow motion, I pedal home.

AN HOUR LATER I am hunched over my plate of porkchops, new potatoes (with their skins, since Mom says that is the healthiest part), applesauce, and peas. Good old Mom, she doesn't ever forget a food group. Once at Arlene's we had goat cheese omelets, strawberry jam, and bagels for dinner. Arlene's dad spent the whole meal talking with great enthusiasm about Viola and Sebastian, the twins from Shakespeare's play *Twelfth Night*, which is one of the things that gave us the idea to write about twins in the first place.

Mom and I aren't looking at each other. When I got home from Arlene's, she said, "Carly, please set the table," while looking at the utensils, and I said, "I poured the milk," while looking at the counter. The department store bag is still in the middle of my bed.

Just before we sit down to dinner, I'm standing by the bookcase in the front hall, trying to see if there are pretty people in adult books, and Dad thinks I'm not listening and tells Mom about a patient of his who has to have an eye removed because of cancer. Mom gasps, because she knows Mrs. Greenberg. Her son, Josh, is a friend of Matt's. Dad explains that Josh's mom is very lucky, because the cancer was caught early. He referred her to one specialist who will remove her eye, and another specialist who will make a false eye for her. My heart sort of lurches. I touch my own eyelid and feel the rounded surface of the eye sliding underneath. I can't imagine what it would be like to have only one eye. Mom's and Dad's voices drop, and I can't hear any more of what they are saying.

A few minutes later Mom calls us to dinner, and as soon as we sit down, we plunge into the dreaded topic: extracurricular activities.

"Jake, I suggested to Carly that she might like to work on the school newspaper or the yearbook," Mom says. "They also have a video club and a Young Scientists Club."

Dad studies his porkchop. Sometimes it's hard to get his attention after he has an especially tough case. Matt steals an opportunity to balance a pea on one tine of his fork and flip it into my milk. Neither Mom nor Dad sees.

"Earth to Jake." Mom cocks her head and stares at Dad.

"I'm sorry. What, Bev?" Dad looks up. "I'm still thinking about my patient, sorry."

"I said, I've been talking to Carly about how important it is to get involved in extracurricular activities."

"Oh, right. It's never too early." Dad smiles at me, glancing at Mom. "Your mother was statewide winner of the science fair two years in a row. And I bet you kids didn't know that she was also homecoming queen."

"You told us," I say.

"Lots of times," adds Matt.

"Well," says Mom with a smile and a glance at Dad, "I bet your dad never told you that he was valedictorian of his high-school *and* his college class."

"Yes, he did," say Matt and I together.

"Well," says Dad, "when it comes to science and math, you kids are really under the gun. European and Asian students have been leaving the Americans in the dust for years."

"We know," we say.

"You kids need to drink your milk," says Mom.

"Yeah, Carly, you *should* drink your milk," says Matt with a grin.

I neatly catapult a pea into Matt's milk. A tiny, white wave licks the edge of the glass.

Mom's and Dad's jaws drop.

"Carly Lewis, what do you think you're doing, shooting peas across the table?"

I feel the blood drain out of my face. "Matt did it first!"

"Carly, go to your room," says Dad. "Now."

I always get caught. Matt never does. I stomp back to my room.

"Matt, is that true, did you flip a pea into Carly's milk?" I hear Dad's voice float down the hall.

"Well . . ."

"Then you go to your room, too. Good grief."

"O.K., Dad," says Matt as he heads in my direction. "We'll let you and Mom have a little peas and quiet. Get it? Peas and quiet? Peace and quiet?"

"In your room, Matt," says Mom, but she's laughing.

When he sees me in the hallway, Matt grins. "I have to admit, that was an excellent shot. For a complete dingleberry."

I slam my door.


CLOSED IN MY ROOM, I rifle through the bag of clothes on the bed and contemplate the unfairness of life. I think about how mad I am at Mom. I'd like to go up to her lab and drown every one of her stupid frogs.

My gray cat, Keesey, meows at the window. Mom doesn't allow her in the house. I open the window, unhook the screen, and let her in. Keesey can't believe her good luck. She rubs up against my leg, her tail quivering with excitement. Then she jumps onto the bed, where she purrs and kneads her claws. She leaves faint, muddy footprints on the pink carpet and small clumps of dirty, gray fur on the pink-and-white-striped bedspread. Mom will be furious.

On my bookshelf is a collection of storybook dolls that my grandmother gave me. They're dressed like characters from literature. Pollyanna. Cleopatra. Wendy from *Peter Pan.* And, the most recent, Jane Austen's Emma. They have blank expressions on their painted faces that give me the creeps.

*You should be grateful that your mother bought you clothes at all,* says Pollyanna.

*You think your life is unfair. I never got to wear anything but a nightgown,* says Wendy.

Lying on my bed, with Keesey as my only companion, I start to cry. At first I cry because Mom and Dad are so unfair. Then I think of other reasons to cry, such as looking like Mr. Potato Head and having to make good grades.

And then I cry about being an ordinary person born into my family instead of a mermaid family or Arlene's. Pretty soon almost anything I think about seems like a reason to cry. I left my favorite stuffed bear at camp. Matt stole my Carolina Tar Heels T-shirt and told Mom it was his, and she believed him. Keesey is four years old and might only live ten or fifteen more years.

*She needs her mommy,* Wendy says.

*Her mummy?* asks Cleopatra.

I look in the mirror at my splotchy face and swollen eyes and cry some more. I finally stop when my head throbs too hard to move it and my nose is so stopped up I have to breathe through my mouth. I'm lying on the bed gasping for air in this way when Mom comes into the room. Keesey, who knows Mom will put her back out, dives under the bed.

"Carly, sweetie?" She sits beside me and rubs my back. "Do you want to talk about it?" Mom's fingers are cool and gentle but also very strong. She can open the most stubborn jar, shake dirt out of the heaviest rug, and lift mattresses with ease.

I try to mumble, "No," but my nose is so stopped up, it comes out "Doe."

"Are you sure?"

"Yes." Muffled into the pillow, I can't talk to her, because I might start crying again, and I already have what feels like lightning bolts of pain shooting through my eyes.

"What is it, sweetie? Did you think I was pressuring you about getting involved? I just know that you have so much to offer, and sometimes I think you hide it because you're shy. I know how competitive the world is now."

I feel my shoulders tense up as she talks, but I don't answer. She waits patiently for a long time, stroking my back with her strong fingers. Finally she leans down, squeezes my shoulders really hard, and whispers, "I love you," into my ear and leaves the room.

Mom and Dad don't understand that it doesn't matter whether I join the video-production team or the newspaper staff or the Young Scientists Club—there are always going to be people smarter and better and prettier and funnier and *whatever* than me. The world has changed since they were young. They want me to be a star, like they were. And I'm not. I'll never be like the models in the magazines or the teens on TV, either. What does that mean? According to Arlene, it means I have character. So why don't I believe her?

I used to be so happy, pretending I was mermaid royalty. Then I could be secretly special. Now I realize that if anybody knew about that stuff (other than Arlene, of course), they would *really* make fun of me.

I take out a copy of the chapter Arlene and I wrote this afternoon and lie on the bed to reread it. Keesey's nose and glowing eyes peek out from under the bed skirt. Then she glides from under the bed and curls up at my feet.

# chapter 4

## The Banyan Tree

DA SPENT HIS NIGHTS watching and recording the nearly imperceptible movements of the stars in the Age of Leo. He counted the years by the seasonal rising of the Dog Star, Sirius, the months by the phases of the moon, and found due north by the star Vega. Every night for the past month, he had seen something in the sky that frightened him. He felt he must warn the king and queen.

In the gray-misted hour before dawn, Da took one cautious step down from the peak of the towering pyramid, and then another. He had not left his observatory for over a year. No one had asked his opinion about anything since he'd predicted the drought last summer. And look what had happened. Nothing but rain. People outside the soothsayer business just didn't know how devastating a small mistake could be.

When Da finally reached the bottom of the pyramid's steep steps, the sun had begun to rise. He almost collapsed. A young man caught him as he stumbled.

"Sir, you look tired. Sit down, and I will get you a drink of water."

Da gratefully sat down and drank the water the young man offered. With a cloth, Da wiped a stray lock of white hair back from his pale, bony forehead.

"Where are you going, sir?" asked the young man.

"I have an urgent warning for the king and queen," said Da. His voice sounded like a crow's, cracked from lack of use.

"What an amazing coincidence," said the young man. "My name is Talar. I'm the junior scribe at the palace, and I'm on my way to work. I can take you there."

The old man squinted at the young scribe. Da had been watching stars for so long, he was out of practice reading faces. The face he saw now was lean and intelligent, and he hoped it was also one he could trust.

Talar allowed Da to lean on his arm as he led the old man past the racecourse. Da gripped the top of his cane, where a strange, gray, triangular stone was embedded in the wood. This was a thunder stone. Legend said that when the thunder stone turned red, catastrophe was near.

"By looking at the stars, I can often foretell the weather to help the farmers and the sailors," Da explained as they walked. "I can predict the phases of the moon and the movements of the ocean's tides. I can predict both solar and lunar eclipses. Sometimes, I can predict drought."

"Of course, sir."

They walked in silence past the high, white, stone walls of the bullfighting arena.

"You are not pale and thin like most scribes," observed Da.

"No, sir." Talar explained that he had left his life in the country as a shepherd and had been writing hieroglyphics in the palace now for just a few months. His job was to make three separate copies of the history of Atlantis. He had very little free time. As soon as he had finished recording the third copy of an event, it always seemed that another event had taken place. He was over a century behind and didn't see how he would ever catch up.

In front of the temple, King Avalach's circular palace slowly rotated so that, once each day, the king and queen could view their entire kingdom. The central atrium was open-air, flanked on one side by the dining hall and the state room and on the other by the family's living quarters. The king and queen had an enormous private bath. All of the baths in Atlantis had hot and cold running water. Bathing was very important to the queen—she had even had baths installed on the roadways for the various types of domestic animals. There were separate baths for horses, bulls, cows, goats, dogs, and cats. (The baths for the cats, as might be guessed, were always empty.)

"This is the children's wing," said Talar as they passed a terra-cotta archway leading to a courtyard containing a sparkling fountain with golden nymphs. There was shouting inside, and a carved, two-handled vase sailed out a palace window and smashed on the tile walkway.

"The young princes fight amongst themselves quite a bit, I hear," added Talar apologetically. "The young princesses, though . . . that's another matter."

"You know them?" Da asked.

"I—" Talar stopped himself. "No, not really." On his second day at the palace, he'd met Eva in a way he would never forget. He had been riding his donkey to work, seen an enchanting girl with wild hair and almond eyes leaving the royal stables, and couldn't help himself—he followed her. He lost her in the maze of courtyards and was turning back when she stepped boldly from behind an olive tree, a ruby-tipped arrow poised in her golden bow.

"Who are you, and why are you following me?"

"Don't shoot!" Talar threw his arms high to show he wasn't armed. Slowly, without taking his eyes off Eva, he swung one long leg over the donkey's ears and slid a few inches to the ground.

"Your Highness, I'm Talar," he said, nervously bowing

while keeping his hands in the air and his eyes on her arrow. "The junior royal scribe. You can trust me."

"How do I know?"

"I work for your father."

"A perfect reason *not* to trust you, from my point of view."

Talar had finally convinced her to lower her bow by promising to teach her and her twin sister to read. Girls in Atlantis, even princesses, weren't supposed to learn to read. He had agreed to teach them, secretly, so each day the tawny girls came to him, with their almond eyes and exquisite ears, one with wild hair and the other's neatly braided, and he gave them reading lessons in a small, out-of-the-way courtyard. The girls brought gifts in exchange for the lessons—gold coins, jewelry, and seashells. They had been quick-witted and learned fast. But Talar was afraid to reveal this secret— even to the wise man.

He led Da to the entrance of the Temple of Poseidon, whose walls shone with gold, silver, and orichalcum. The outside portico was lined with white marble columns, and through the twenty-foot doors a gigantic golden statue of Poseidon riding a chariot almost touched the domed ceiling of the main hall. Around him were a hundred gold statues of sea nymphs riding on dolphins.

"There are a great many more gold statues than I remember," commented Da. The reflections made his eyes water.

"Yes, the king and queen are quite fond of them," Talar responded.

When they reached the throne room, Talar led Da forward and quickly bowed. "Your Highnesses, I have brought Da, the astronomer, with an urgent warning." Talar didn't understand why everyone in the room began to laugh.

As his nose touched the floor, Talar caught sight of Eva and Lydia crawling slowly behind the thrones. They darted behind a tapestry, and he watched their jeweled feet tiptoe along the wall behind it.

Talar wondered why the princesses were hiding in the throne room. Backing into the doorway, he spread his cape wide as he bowed once more, remaining in that position for as long as he dared. This allowed the two girls to run out the door behind him, seen only by Da, who slightly raised one white eyebrow.

As Talar turned, he glimpsed the girls running down the open-air corridor. They stopped for an instant, and Lydia smiled while Eva's lips formed the words *thank you*. Then the princesses sprinted across the temple yard toward the royal stables.

Talar sighed. Surely the beautiful and fearless Eva would want a man of action, not a scribe who bent over clay tablets all day.

"Tell us your urgent message," the queen was saying to Da.

"Yes, what's going on in the heavens these days?" asked King Avalach, with a superior smile. "I've been somewhat busy here on earth and haven't had much time lately to look up."

Da pretended he didn't see the mathematician, the priest, or the engineer chuckling and exchanging glances. The king and queen descended from their thrones of polished stone, with golden Poseidon towering behind them, and indicated that Da should stroll with them around the fountain. The engineer, the mathematician, and the priest followed along. Two slaves cleaning a minute amount of algae from the statues quietly moved to another part of the fountain when the king and queen approached.

Spots of light leaped from the fountain and the gleaming statues. Tears welled in Da's eyes, which were so accustomed to darkness. The splashing water seemed suddenly to roar in his ears like a tidal wave crashing, and he felt faint and confused.

Da spoke solemnly, steadying himself on his walking stick. The gray stone in the handle faintly glowed. "There is a star in the heavens that grows each day. I have seen a vision of destruction. You should build a ship and fit it with enough supplies to begin life anew. Save your people and the memory of Atlantis."

King Avalach's ceremonial ankus sliced the air. "Atlantis destroyed?"

"That's absurd!" Queen Lannu gestured so abruptly that a golden bracelet flew from her wrist into the fountain. One of the servants dove to retrieve it.

"Your soothsaying has lacked the ring of truth for years, old man." The king snorted. "Have you noticed, for instance, how *dry* it's been as of late?" He pointed his ankus at the trembling slave, now soaking wet, who offered the bracelet to the queen. "Do not touch the jewelry of the queen unless ordered to do so!"

The queen tore the bracelet from the servant's hand.

Da repeated his message in a quiet voice. "I have seen the signs clearly. Atlantis will be destroyed."

"Get rid of him!" shouted King Avalach. Two bodyguards stepped forward and grabbed Da's thin arms. "Old man, you are hereby banished to the top of the pyramid forever! I forbid you to show your face in the city of Atlantis again!"

Talar's eyes met Da's as the bodyguards hauled the old man from the throne room.

"You must finish your history," Da croaked to the young scribe. "Bring it to the top of the pyramid by midnight tomorrow."

Talar could only nod, open-mouthed. Finish a century of history in two days? The old man must be dreaming.

\*       \*       \*

"FORGET THE SADDLES. WE'LL ride bareback," Eva whispered. She tiptoed into the stall of her favorite black mare, Sphinx, and with the flat of her hand pushed the bit between the horse's teeth. Lydia's silver mare, Nya, tossed her head but finally allowed Lydia to slide the bridle over her ears.

Eva lay down close to Sphinx's neck as she urged her mount silently out into the early morning mist. Lydia followed on Nya. The only sound was the swish of Nya's nervous tail.

The two mares cantered past the palace gardens and the servant quarters. Lydia didn't have to ask where they were going. She knew. As their rhyme said, "Your thoughts are my thoughts . . . your heart is my heart." Many stadia outside the royal grounds, she and Eva had a secret hiding place among the branches of an eighty-foot banyan tree. This enormous tree had a gnarled, ropy trunk so thick that seven children could stretch their arms around it as far as they could and still not touch fingertips. The tree's gigantic umbrella-shaped canopy of leaves cast a shadow three hundred feet wide.

Just then Lydia received a mental message from Eva that seemed to be I TOO FEW TARRY THE PLAIN CLOD! She rode along behind Eva for several dozen yards or so, trying to figure out what this might mean, until Eva turned in her saddle and cleared up the confusion. "I refuse to marry the rain god!" she declared. Then she kissed the air behind Sphinx's left ear and dug her heels into the mare's sides. Sphinx gathered herself and broke into a gallop.

Lydia hesitated. Her heart did a flip-flop. "Wait for me!" she finally shouted. Nya was used to following Sphinx and leaped forward with barely a nudge.

The two horses, black and silver, waded the swollen river and streaked through the rising curls of fog in the royal vineyards. In the fallow fields beyond, long, green grass swished and crackled against the horses' legs. The sky was a throbbing blue, and singing grasshoppers flung about through the hot air. To the west, in the distance, a thin, white plume strayed from the tip of the volcano. The girls crossed the ridge. Sphinx and Nya's hoofs rang on the rocky trail.

As morning wore into afternoon and they descended to the grasslands below, a low growl of thunder rumbled in the distance. A black storm cloud rolled toward them.

"Head for the banyan tree!" Eva shouted. They reached its enormous, sheltering limbs moments before the black cloud unleashed the rains. The girls tethered their horses, quickly found handholds and toeholds on the gigantic trunk, and swung up into the lower limbs of the tree to wait out the storm.

"The boys are probably having supper with Mom and Dad about now," said Lydia. Once a week the children were required to join the king and queen at dinner. The royal dining table was one hundred feet long and made from the trunk of a four-hundred-year-old eucalyptus tree. It was so long that the king and queen, who sat at opposite ends, had to shout through a ram's horn to converse with each other. The boys sat to the king's right and the girls to the king's left. As the bowls of grapes, lamb chops, and couscous made their way around, the children's parents would grill them on what they had learned the previous week. The boys were being taught history, mathematics, and philosophy. Eva and Lydia were being taught how to sew and play the lyre.

"Last week I almost gave away our secret lessons with Talar," said Eva. Talar wasn't a bad-looking fellow, really, although he didn't have much in the way of muscles. Still, he had a gentle manner about him that Eva sort of liked.

"I know," said Lydia. "You were about to correct Atlan

when he forgot the names of the first rulers of Atlantis. Thank Poseidon no one noticed."

"I only got away with it because Aenean started throwing grapes in our goat milk, and then Andros gave his entire dinner to the dog, and Mother got annoyed, remember?"

"And then Aidan kicked me under the table. I still have a bruise on my shin." Lydia balanced her heel on the branch and poked gently at the purple spot. "Oh, I almost forgot." She drew a small, copper mirror from her pocket. It was ornately decorated and appeared to be very old. "Look."

"Where did you find it?" Eva examined the mirror, which was perfectly round, had no handle, and was small enough to fit in the palm of her hand.

"Under that table where we were hiding, with the scepters and crowns. Tomorrow we better sneak into the throne room again so I can put it back. The strange thing is, when you look at yourself in the mirror, there's nothing there. See?" Lydia held the mirror in front of her own face. The surface remained shiny and blank.

Eva looked at herself in the glass, and her image sprang into focus, blindingly bright. "Yes, there is. Look."

Lydia peered over Eva's shoulder. There Eva was. But over her shoulder, where Lydia should have been, was a blank surface. "Why does the mirror show you but not me?"

Eva shrugged. "Maybe it's the light or the angle or something. We are not marrying any drippy old rain god," she added fiercely.

Lydia put the mirror back into her pocket. The rain tapped a tattoo on the leaves above, and a stray drop of water rolled into the hollow of her collarbone. "What can we do?"

"We've already done it," Eva said. "We've run away."

# chapter 5

## *Forces of Nature*

THE FIRST DAY OF school, I discovered that Arlene and I didn't have the same lunch period. I had to eat by myself. It was so embarrassing that I have no idea what I ate, plus I got lost trying to find my next class in spite of the fact that it was my second year in this school.

My locker is ancient and dented and has been painted many times. The top coat is a sickly yellowish green. Someone wrote "Darryl loves Cindy" on the inside of the door. I wonder who Darryl and Cindy are, if they are still in middle school, or if they are already in high school or even college. Does Darryl still love Cindy? Or are they going out with other people? This school is pretty old. Maybe they're married and have little kids who go to my elementary school. Or maybe they're grandparents by now and live together in a little two-room apartment at Whispering Pines Retirement Village off Peacehaven Road.

A group of popular girls meets here right next to my locker before homeroom every day. They have high, trilling laughs and wear cool clothes, and when they talk, they act like everyone is watching them. Which they are.

On the first day of school, Arlene and I passed this group, and two girls—one with a blond ponytail and one with long, dark hair—peeled away from the group and started walking behind us. I glanced back, and the blond was imitating Arlene's knock-kneed gait and arm waving. The dark-haired girl was walking in a timid shuffle and looking up at the other one adoringly. I guess that was supposed to be me. The rest of the group hooted with laughter. Arlene didn't notice. I pretended not to, but my face was flaming hot.

I guess I'd pictured Arlene and me going everywhere together, and it came as sort of a shock that Arlene is in only one of my classes, advanced language arts. We have Miss Norden, who is really young and enthusiastic. She doesn't call us "boys and girls" as the other teachers do. She says, "All right, people. Eyes up front, people." She is not much taller than I am, with short, dark hair, and she even wears jeans sometimes. She might be pretty if she didn't look so stern. She always has two vertical creases on her forehead, and her eyes behind her wire-rim glasses are green and intense. She lectures about point of view and says, "And an example of that is *The Outsiders*. How many of you have read that book?" We all stare at her blankly except for Zack Wingo, who barely raises the ends of his fingers. He just moved here from California and sits in the back row drawing these fabulous, intricate cartoons that look like superheroes battling strange monsters from mythology—half-dragon, half-unicorn or half-bull, half-man. Zack is different from the North Carolina guys. He acts like he's heard and read everything before. He is on the cross-country team, and the second day of school, on the way to the bus, I saw him standing by his locker wearing black running shorts. He has lean muscles in his thighs.

Miss Norden puts her hands on her hips and says, "I'd like to start out by assigning the first three chapters of *The Outsiders* for the end of the week."

Marty Bellows, a short guy with thick glasses who always sits in the first row, raises his hand and says, "Is this for a grade?" And Miss Norden stares at him over the tops of her wire rims and says, "Yes, Marty, this is for a grade."

Part of me desperately hopes I will be Miss Norden's pet, while another part of me knows that will automatically make the rest of the kids in the class hate me. But on the second day of school, Miss Norden calls out Arlene's last name during roll call and looks up quickly to connect Arlene's face with her name.

"Is your father the lit professor at the college, Arlene?"

"Yes, ma'am."

"Oh, I took every class he taught. He is my *idol*. Is he still crazy about Jane Austen?"

"Yes, ma'am, he sure is. Jane is such a *wit*, you know." Arlene fakes an English accent and grins. Miss Norden giggles. The other kids in the class roll their eyes. I am briefly terrified that Arlene will make me do the scene from *Sense and Sensibility* again. The level of embarrassment I experienced in front of her family would be nothing compared to the entire language arts class. I'm thankful that Arlene simply exchanges a few pleasantries about British literature with Miss Norden and does not bring up our acting ability.

Now we all know Arlene will be Miss Norden's pet. The truth is, she'll be the best student, and she'll deserve it. I guess I'll have to be happy with being Arlene's sidekick. Which is slightly better than being a complete nonentity, I guess.

AFTER CAREFUL CONSIDERATION, I'VE decided to join the Young Scientists Club. It only meets once a month, therefore will require a minimum of effort, and hopefully will get Mom off my back. I go to the first meeting, which is before school on Tuesday of the following week. Four people show up. Marty Bellows, because his parents want him to be premed and make him join everything. Craig Weisener, whose dad is the mayor. A shy, pudgy girl named Amy Chu, who is in my language arts class and writes poetry in tiny, crabbed handwriting. And me. I was going to ask Arlene to join, but in all the confusion of school starting, I forgot.

The adviser is Mr. Allen, the seventh-grade earth science teacher. He is short and very young, with blond hair that curls at his temples. He doesn't look much older than some of the eighth-grade boys, except he always wears a tie. A lot of the girls have crushes on him. Once in the bathroom I heard one girl tell another, with raised eyebrows, "He has a very extensive vocabulary." Someone else told me that once, when he was teaching a unit on the movement of tectonic plates, he threw a chair across the room.

Mr. Allen looks at his watch and says, "Well, let's wait a few more minutes. Some people may have gotten hung up." But no one else comes, so he finally starts the meeting with just the four of us.

Instead of telling us to be quiet, Mr. Allen says, "Chill, folks." He acts very formal with us, though. He calls me "Ms. Lewis" instead of Carly. Someone saw him wearing an earring when they ran into him at the grocery store, but he doesn't wear it in school.

Marty raises his hand at the beginning to ask if we can get extra credit in science for being in this club.

"Oh, you can take it to the bank," says Mr. Allen.

"Really?" says Marty, his eyes brightening.

"No, Mr. Bellows, I'm being facetious." Apparently *facetious* is one of Mr. Allen's favorite words. I wish I knew what it meant. As if he's read my mind, Mr. Allen says, "Who knows what *facetious* means?"

"It means you're joking," says Amy in a tiny voice.

"That is correct, Ms. Chu!" says Mr. Allen. "I'm sure each and every one of you joined this club for the love of science, not just to get another extracurricular activity to put on your transcript."

I scan the faces for one person who might actually be here for the love of science. I think maybe thirty years ago my mother would have been here for that. We pass around a sheet of paper and write down our e-mail addresses and phone numbers so Mr. Allen can notify us about stuff.

"Let me tell you about our first project," says Mr. Allen. "We're going to put together a time line of natural disasters—"

"By natural disasters—you mean earthquakes and volcanoes and stuff?" interrupts Marty.

"That's the ticket," says Mr. Allen. "Fascinating stuff, huh?"

"Cool," says Marty.

"It can be a notorious earthquake," Mr. Allen continues, "a volcanic eruption, a major hurricane or typhoon, a tsunami—does everyone know what that is?"

"A tidal wave," says Marty.

"That is correct, Mr. Bellows," says Mr. Allen. "A meteor striking the earth can also qualify as a natural disaster. I'd like to post this time line on the school Web site. Everyone who contributes will get to go on a very awesome science club field trip. In mid-November there's going to be an outstanding meteor shower called the Leonids. Has anybody heard of it?"

"I have!" Marty's hand shoots toward the ceiling like a space shuttle taking off from Cape Canaveral. "It's a meteor shower that peaks every thirty-three years. It looks like it's coming from the constellation of Leo. But that's an optical illusion. And there can be more than a hundred thousand shooting stars per hour."

Mr. Allen gives a tiny smile. "Excellent, Mr. Bellows," he says and sits on his desk. "Sky watchers have known about the Leonids since before Egyptian times. The Leonid meteor storm in the year 1833 was so incredible that many people believed the end of the world was coming. That storm inspired the first scientific study of meteors. The Leonids are at their most spectacular every thirty-three years or so, as Mr. Bellows said, when the earth passes through trails of dust left by the comet Tempel-Tuttle."

"This year they're supposed to be fantastic!"

"That is correct, Mr. Bellows," said Mr. Allen. "They're predicting the Leonids will be especially good here on the east coast. I've already gotten permission for our club to go on a field trip to Pilot Mountain in the middle of November. Anyone who researches and writes up a disaster for the time line can go. Spread the word. Tell everybody you know that the Young Scientists Club is having a field trip where you get to stay up all night. Any questions?"

"Can we get extra credit in language arts for our disaster write-ups?"

Marty again. Mr. Allen sighs and rubs his hands over his face.

BY FRIDAY OF THE second week of school, I am starting to feel like I hate the world. I don't know why I feel so blah. I'm going over to Arlene's after school, and we plan to write until midnight. Normally I would count the minutes until I could run through her scraggy front yard with her mom's collection of birdbaths and hummingbird feeders, and up, up the cluttered stairs to the third-floor room with the stars on the ceiling. But today, trying to feel excited about anything seems like too much trouble. I ask Miss Norden for a hall pass because my stomach hurts. This is a big mistake.

Miss Norden has already spelled out her rules on using the rest room in the middle of class. "You're not preschoolers, you know," she said on the first day, looking at us wide-eyed through her glasses. "There will be no hall passes given out this period. Period."

So when I ask for the hall pass, she cocks her head and looks at me with narrowed eyes. She thinks I'm *lying*. But my stomach really does hurt; I have a hot liquid ache that reaches all the way to my knees. Then, suddenly, her eyes flicker with something like kindness, and she hands me a hall pass.

"Don't make a habit of it." She turns away. "O.K., people, let's talk about voice in *The Outsiders*."

I try to catch Arlene's eye as I leave, but she is raising her hand to answer a question Miss Norden hasn't even finished asking.

My tennis shoes make a squeaking sound on the green linoleum as I walk down the empty hall. The bathroom door creaks as I push it open. I hear sounds like rats scurrying, followed by a giggle. A toilet flushes. Choking billows of ash gray smoke curl from behind a stall door, and a popular girl shoves past me, popping a breath mint into her mouth.

Someone else is still smoking in one of the stalls, so I go into one at the far end of the row. When I discover clumps of brownish red blood on my underpants, I gasp.

"Oh no." My heart wrenches itself into a knot and skips a beat. Sweat pops out on my forehead. My stomach cramps.

"What's wrong?" says a fakey Southern voice from the smoky stall.

I feel foolish talking to a voice whose owner I can't see and don't know. "I started my period," I finally say in a choked voice.

"Oh, you must be bumming." I hear the end of a cigarette sizzle, and the toilet flushes. "It didn't leak through, did it?"

I quickly look at my khakis. There's a spot about an inch in diameter. "Oh no." Did everyone in the class see it? I feel like I'm going to throw up.

"Here you go." A hand pokes under the stall with a tampon. The fingers have purple glitter nail polish. Under the metal stall door I can see that she wears jeans and a pair of those elevator shoes Mom won't let me get because she says I'll break my ankle.

"Thanks," I whisper. I take the slender cylinder in its crackly, hygienic white paper. Mom said she would show me how to use one. But we haven't gotten around to it.

"Here." The purple fingernails slide a tie-dyed T-shirt like the ones the girls are wearing this year under the stall door. "Wear it around your waist."

"Thanks." I figure I won't need it long since I plan to go right to the office and call Mom, but I take it anyway.

"I'm Whitney." Paper tears, and a pencil rasps. "Here's my number. I'm in Mrs. Rohrbach's homeroom. Just bring the T-shirt back Monday, or whenever. Good luck, O.K.?"

The fingernails of my benefactor appear under the stall door once again with a scrap of paper that has "Whitney Sullivan" and a phone number written on it. The door creaks as she leaves the bathroom. And suddenly I have a new friend with purple fingernails and a tie-dyed T-shirt. We have shared the secret of womanhood. Only I have never seen her face, and she has never seen mine.

WHEN I GET HOME from school, Mom is sitting at the dining room table with her laptop and about ten separate drafts of her grant proposal, all with big X's and scribbling and various charts and graphs. Her hair needs to be washed, and mascara is smeared under her eyes like the stuff they put under football players' eyes to protect from glare. She has algae smeared on her sleeve. She looks me over.

"Where did you get that shirt?" Whitney's T-shirt is tied around my waist. "And why are you walking funny?"

I have been keeping my knees sort of together as I walk because I'm afraid the tampon might fall out. I took so long in the bathroom I never even made it back to Miss Norden's class.

"I started my period." I say it quietly but dramatically and drop my backpack on the floor. Mom does exactly what I want her to do. She drops her pen and jumps to her feet. Her hands fly to her mouth.

"Oh, Carly!" Her eyes suddenly look swimmy and bright. She takes two big steps and wraps her arms around me. I am trying not to cry.

"Why didn't you call me?"

"I did. You were in a lecture."

She breathes, "I'm so sorry, sweetie," into my hair. She strokes my head again and again, and I wish she would never stop.

The garage door grinds open, which means Dad and Matt are home from soccer practice.

"It's no big deal," I say, pulling away. Whitney's phone number is folded in my pocket, and I check to make sure I haven't lost it. But it doesn't really matter since I have it memorized.

Dad and Matt come in from the garage. Dad's keys clatter on the counter, and Matt's soccer ball and shoes bang into the back wall of the hall closet.

"So did you see all my headers, Dad?" Matt sits on the floor and peels off his sweat-soaked socks and shin guards.

"Pee-you!" I say. Matt responds by throwing a sock at my face.

"Absolutely, " Dad says. His white medical jacket is folded over his arm, and his tie dangles loose. "Good job. The coach thought you were really hustling out there." Matt grins as he reaches into the refrigerator for a sports drink.

"Use a glass!" Mom says, but it's too late. Matt has chugged out of the bottle. "I read an article about headers just last week," she adds when Matt wipes off the lip of the bottle and hands it to Dad. "Hitting the ball with your head like that can cause brain damage. I want you to stop it, Matt."

"Yeah," I say. "You might damage your one brain cell." I pick up my backpack and trudge down the hall to my room.

"LOL. Dingleberry." Matt hurls another sweaty sock at me.

"I'll be right there, sweetie," Mom calls.

Mom comes in a minute later as I am lying on my bed idly thinking, for some reason, about Zack Wingo's leg muscles. She sits down next to me with a plastic bag containing an assortment of feminine products.

"I bought these for you a few months ago. Do you want to try them and see which ones you like? I could help you with that right now." Mom strokes my arm for a minute, then glances at her watch. "I have about half an hour before I need to go inject some tadpoles with dye. Do you want me to take you to Arlene's on the way?" Her brows are knitted, and I can tell she feels guilty about leaving me but doesn't know what else to do.

I sigh. "I guess I'll go to Arlene's."

ARLENE IS ON THE floor, trying to do that yoga pose where you point your legs up in the air and elevate your entire torso except for your head and shoulders. I am sitting at her desk, typing. My stomach aches dully. Even though I haven't said a word to Arlene, I feel like I have a huge sign around my neck that says I JUST GOT MY PERIOD.

We've finished writing about the wise man Da, who is warning people that Atlantis will be destroyed, only everyone thinks he's crazy. Arlene says when we write about Da, she thinks of her grandfather, who is tall and stooped with a white beard and paints very bad paintings. I think about mine, who is short and bald and plays golf every day and participates in Civil War reenactments on the weekends. I like the idea that we created one character from two completely different people.

"So now what?" I say. I yank my hair into a ponytail, then let it fall onto my shoulders. "Talar is in love with Eva, which means we need to come up with someone for Lydia."

*"Actually,"* says Arlene. The upside-down yoga position smushes her rib cage so her voice sounds cartoony when she talks. "Shakespeare never allows people to be in love with each other. Person A is always in love with Person B, who's in love with Person C, who's in love with Person A. Another cardinal rule about twins in Shakespeare is that people in love with them always get them mixed up."

I've wondered about that. I think that surely there would be some tiny little mole or mannerism that would give away which twin was which. If I had a clone, wouldn't Mom or Dad somehow know it wasn't me? If a boy, say Zack Wingo, for example, were to fall madly in love with me, and he was truly in love, how could he ever mistake me for someone else? I once asked Arlene why the parents in *The Parent Trap* took so long to figure out which twin they had, and she said with a shrug, "Carly, if they had known right away, there would have been no story."

Now I focus on the stars spilling across Arlene's ceiling. "What about Eva and Lydia? Let's say each of them falls in love with a guy who's in love with her sister."

Arlene slowly lowers her shoulders and back, vertebra by

vertebra, then her bottom, to the floor. She stares at her elevated feet, points and flexes them, then sits up and twirls a piece of stringy hair around her index finger. "Did Wilbur fall in love with Charlotte? Of course not."

"Well, Fern *did* sort of start liking Henry what's-his-name." This is the first time I've challenged Arlene's superior knowledge of literature.

"Don't you think falling in love is a little too predictable?" Arlene fixes me with an earnest look. "I mean, really."

"I like the falling in love part," I say weakly. Predictable? I can't predict whether Zack will ever even look in my direction, much less notice my existence. Falling in love seems, to me, to be the most unpredictable thing in the entire world.

We spend most of the night arguing. We argue about what to name a new character who can fly. I want to name him "Orville" or "Wilbur" after the Wright Brothers. Arlene insists that Leonardo da Vinci *"actually"* was one of the first to invent a flying machine. Finally, we name our character after all three. We argue some more about love, and I sneak some in.

When it's time to go to bed, instead of just changing in front of her the way I usually do, I carefully get my things together and go downstairs to the bathroom Arlene shares with Juliet. Arlene gives me a funny look, but I pretend I don't see. I change my tampon the way Mom showed me, then carefully smooth my nightgown before going back upstairs. I get into bed and pull the covers to my neck.

"We need more magic in our book," says Arlene in the dark. "How about if the twins are clairvoyant as children, but they lose their clairvoyance as they get older? Or, I know— telekinesis. You know, being able to make things move just by thinking about it?"

I'm sleepy. My stomach hurts, and I have a headache. Arlene and her magic are a million miles away.

# CHAPTER 6

# *The Flying Man*

EVA AND LYDIA AWOKE the following morning, wet and stiff inside the green-shrouded room formed by the drooping branches of the banyan tree. Nya and Sphinx were grazing a few yards away, and the tree was completely surrounded by a wild mastodon herd. Their hairy trunks swung in a contented rhythm, and their gigantic ivory tusks gleamed in the morning sun. The clouds had blown away, and the sky pulsed bright blue.

Eva threaded a red ant from her wild locks and placed it gently on the tree trunk. "Hey, I've got an idea. Let's try to ride a mastodon."

"A mastodon? You're kidding, right?" Lydia decided if Eva tried to ride a mastodon, she'd scream at the top of her lungs to scare away the beasts.

"You better not try to scare them away," Eva said suddenly.

"Did you just read my mind?"

Eva's eyes opened wide. "I did, didn't I?"

"We're getting better."

"Pretty soon we'll be able to converse without saying a word."

Lydia shifted her weight from one sore haunch to another. "Anyway, Mom and Dad would kill us if they found out we were riding mastodons."

"Lydia, Mom and Dad want us to marry Driz, the rain god."

"Mom and Dad love us," Lydia offered weakly. "It's

43

that priest who wants us to marry the rain god. What exactly happens when you marry him?"

"You stand out on Gibraltar Rock in your most gorgeous tunic, wearing every ounce of jewelry you own, and then jump into the ocean."

"And are there lots of people down below in reed boats, playing lyres and waiting to help you out of the water?"

"No. There are lots of waves waiting to smash you up against the rock."

Lydia swallowed. "O.K., well, what the heck, let's ride a mastodon."

Two young mastodons were playing and splashing right below them in a pool by the tree. On her stomach, Eva shimmied out onto a low branch hanging over the pool. She pointed to a nearby branch. She intended for Lydia to swing down and drop about four feet onto the mastodon's back.

As Lydia crawled out, the branch bowed under her weight. The leaves rustled, and she could hear her own nervous breath.

Eva plunged from her branch and hung by her fingers. One of the mastodons trumpeted shrilly, and a sudden voice from above shouted, "Look out!"

A flying man with golden ringlets and white-feathered wings bore down on them out of the sky, his arms and legs flailing. The air filled with the mastodons' trumpets of terror, and the banyan tree shuddered as the massive beasts stampeded out of the pond and across the plain. The flying man clipped the branch where Eva hung and nose-dived into the water, splashing muddy white feathers everywhere. With a scream, Eva fell on top of him.

"My apologies," he said.

"Eva, are you all right?" Lydia slid down the tree and jumped into the pond after her sister. The flying man looked up at her, and his eyes were as blue and free as the sky he had fallen from.

Eva struggled to her feet in the muddy, waist-deep water of the pond. Then the flying man attempted to stand, but the weight of the wet feathers on his huge wings was too much.

"Could one of you possibly untie my wings?" he asked breathlessly.

"So the wings aren't real?" Eva glanced at Lydia. "I thought you were a god flying from the heavens!"

"Me, too!" Lydia examined the way the wings were tied to his wrists and elbows and knotted together across his back. It was difficult, at this awkward angle, for him to look at her, but he twisted his head and smiled. What a smile. She *had* thought him to be nothing less than a god, or a messenger from the gods. There was a whole sky in his eyes. They were too mesmerizing to belong to any ordinary man. She yanked at the knotted leather between the wings, and her hand brushed the sharp edge of his shoulder blade. He was thin, unlike her muscular brothers.

Eva drew her jeweled copper knife. "We're going to have to cut it."

The flying man flinched. "All right. Go ahead." The knife rasped against leather. As soon as Eva had cut him free of the wings, he stood, and the girls helped him drag the stained wings to shore. "Gentle ladies, I owe you my life. My name is Leorbur." He bowed.

"I'm Eva, and this is my twin sister, Lydia."

"A pleasure to meet you." Tenderly, he began laying the wings in the sun to dry. "Look at all the feathers I've lost. All the hours of work." He waded into the shallow water at the edge of the pond and scooped up as many floating feathers as he could. Without thinking, Lydia waded in and helped him.

"My calculations must have been off by a hair." He examined the knots of leather Eva had cut. "Maybe a harness. More bird-watching."

Eva looked at Lydia and made a small, circular motion next to her temple, shorthand for "crazy."

Lydia usually agreed with Eva, but not this time. There was something so pure and intense about this flying man named Leorbur. She didn't think there was anything crazy about him. She gave him the nest of damp feathers she'd collected from the pond, and their hands touched.

"Thank you." His eyes flickered at her, and then he stuffed the stray feathers into a leather pouch tied around his waist. "I must get back to work. I would offer to fly you ladies somewhere, but as you can see, I haven't perfected this flying thing quite yet." He hoisted a dripping wing over each shoulder.

"Can you carry those by yourself?"

"Sure, I do it all the time." Lydia caught one of the wings as it slid off his shoulder. When she pushed it back up, the other one started to slide. Eva caught that one and pushed it up. When he was balanced, they took a step back.

He bowed, thanked them again, and began trudging across the valley toward the far ridge.

"Wait!" Lydia ran after him. "Do you always practice your flying around here?"

He stopped and turned. Lydia jumped back to avoid being smacked in the face with his wings. "Yes, I use the ridge for a running start and glide on the up breezes from the valley. The gliding part is going pretty well. It's just when I try to flap the wings that something goes wrong."

"Well, do you ever need any, um, help?"

"Not really." He blinked and stared at her legs in such an intense way that Lydia wanted to cover them. Then something seemed to occur to him, and he snapped his fingers. "Our legs. We have more power in our legs! That's it!" He strode off purposefully. The muscles in his thighs were long and sinewy.

Lydia called after him. "Maybe we'll see you around."

They watched him head toward the ridge, wading through the yellow grass, the sun shining on his curly, golden head. Small birds darted out of the grass as he approached, and he stopped to watch them fly with rapt concentration.

"What a weirdo," said Eva as she gathered up Sphinx's reins. "There are plenty of things in Atlantis that are supposed to fly. Dragons, birds, butterflies, griffins. But not people."

Lydia didn't answer. She ran the palm of her hand down Nya's smooth, silver neck as she watched Leorbur trudge away. "Well," she said, "which way should we go?"

"There are places to hide in the hills," said Eva.

DA LAY ON HIS back on a stone bench, blanketed by the cool, mysterious fire of the stars in the dark sky. His limbs felt heavy, so very heavy, like stones. He'd had to rest many times during the climb to the top of the pyramid. It did not matter that he could never leave here again. Time was short. His eyes were closed, but in his mind's eye he could see every constellation as it rotated above him around the North Star. The Big Dipper, the Little Dipper, Orion, and Sirius, the Dog Star. And, of course, the two faces of Gemini, the Twins.

He opened his eyes, and the stars rose in the same comforting, winking patterns that had imprinted forever in his memory. Soon there would be a brilliant star in the western sky visible to anyone in Atlantis who chanced to look up.

# chapter 7

# Whitney

ON SUNDAY I CALL Whitney and arrange to meet her near my locker the next day to give back the T-shirt. She's friendly and chatty on the phone, as if she spends hours saying clever things to people.

"My parents are divorced," she says, "just in case you were wondering."

"Oh," I say. "Sorry."

"I tried to run away when I first found out, but now it's no big deal." I can hear music in the background, and Whitney sings along for a little while.

I am practically obsessed with who she might be. I looked at every girl's fingernails in the bus parking lot after school on Friday, trying to find the purple glitter.

On Sunday night I go on-line and get excited for a minute. I've gotten an e-mail from Mr. Allen. I open the mail and see that he's e-mailed everyone in the Young Scientists Club. My screen name (Mermaid12) is one of a list of four. The e-mail says:

> Dear Young Scientists:
>
> Marty Bellows has submitted three entries for our natural-disasters time line and thus is the first on the list for the all-night field trip!! Here they are:
>
> **HUMONGOUS ASTEROID**
> Why did the dinosaurs become extinct? Some scientists believe that a humongous asteroid crashed

into the land that is now Mexico about 65 million years ago, which could explain huge weather changes and maybe even why the dinosaurs became extinct.

## HUMONGOUS COMET

Some scientists believe that around 50,000 B.C. a humongous comet collided with the earth in the region of southwestern North Carolina and created the huge craters we call the Carolina Bays.

## HUMONGOUS FLOOD

Artifacts from 300 feet deep in the Black Sea have been discovered, which is a clue that a humongous flood happened about 7500 B.C., which caused the Mediterranean Sea to rise 300 feet and flood an area the size of Florida. This might even be the flood described in the Bible when Noah built his ark. Or maybe it is the same flood in the Babylonian story of Gilgamesh.

Anybody else interested in going on the all-night field trip to see the Leonids? Send me a natural disaster!
Mr. Allen

Oh brother, I thought. Marty Bellows is a humongous kiss-up.

ON MONDAY I STAND by my locker holding the T-shirt in a plastic bag, waiting for Whitney. I've started to picture her with wild auburn hair, just like Eva in our novel. She has become Eva to me, with almond eyes and slim, tan arms and perfect little ears, of course. It's as if Eva is a paper doll, and I have taken off her tunic and instead dressed her in a tie-dyed T-shirt, jeans, elevator shoes, and purple glitter nail polish. And I, of course, have turned into Lydia, and we are inseparable twins.

The blond-haired girl with the ponytail who imitated Arlene's knock-kneed walk the first day of school comes around the corner. I look away quickly.

But she comes right up to me. "Carly?" she says. I glance at her face. She does have high cheekbones and almond eyes and small ears like seashells, but there the resemblance to Eva ends. She's pretty, but if she narrowed her eyes, she would look mean. I look down. She's wearing elevator shoes. My eyes travel up to meet green nail polish. I breathe a sigh of relief. It's not her.

"I'm Whitney," she says. "Hey."

I blink. "But you had on *purple* glitter nail polish."

She cocks her head, and her sleek, blond ponytail makes a slithery, swishing sound against the nylon of her jacket. She looks puzzled and examines her fingernails. She must think I'm a complete idiot. "Oh, well, yeah, I changed colors over the weekend. Do you like this?" The green is the color of chlorophyll, or a grasshopper. This is Whitney? The kind and generous girl who gave me a tampon is the girl who made fun of Arlene? Her dark-haired friend made fun of me. I can almost hear the dream I've built start to tumble like an avalanche down the side of a mountain.

"My mom washed your T-shirt. I didn't get anything on it, but she still washed it. It's clean." I chatter on, sounding ridiculous, and thrust the bag toward her.

"Oh, listen, don't worry about it. Are you still having it? My first one lasted two weeks." She's talking in a normal tone of voice in the middle of the main hall, and I look around quickly because I'm afraid someone might hear. She wears sweet, heavy perfume, but I can also smell cigarettes. The smell is a little nauseating but exciting at the same time.

"Well, anyway, thanks." I wonder if now that she knows who I am, she'll decide that she'd rather not hang out with me. Maybe she doesn't realize I'm the same person she saw with Arlene. People always notice Arlene. She's tall and waves her arms around, and she's always pushing her glasses back up her nose in an authoritative way. She is always expressing her opinion and doesn't care what anyone thinks. But not too many people notice me.

Whitney's squinting at me with a thoughtful look on her face. Suddenly she reaches out and takes off my glasses. My flimsy wire rims are folded in her celery-tipped fingers. Multicolored blobs go past behind her in the hall. I breathe deeply to keep from panicking.

"You know," she says, "you're really quite pretty without your glasses."

"What?" I squeak.

"Meet me in the bathroom last period, and I'll give you a makeover." She slides the glasses back onto my nose, and her broad, mischievous grin comes into focus. Behind her Zack is standing at his locker with his back to us. He runs his fingers through his hair, trying to decide which books he needs, I guess. There are freckles on the back of his hand, and the edge of his pinky and the heel of his palm are coated shiny gray with graphite from drawing cartoons all the time.

"See ya!" Whitney has taken her T-shirt, and she's gone. I should not even think about leaving Miss Norden's class again today. I could end up in detention. As far as Mom and Dad are concerned, I might as well get sent to Alcatraz.

"O.K., CLOSE YOUR EYES." I do. I'm standing on top of a toilet with Whitney so that if any teachers come into the bathroom to look for us, they won't see our feet. We lean on the metal walls of the stall, facing each other, and she is making up my face.

I hold my breath and listen for the door squealing open or brisk adult footsteps in the hall as the eye shadow brush pricks against my eyelids. I can smell Whitney's musky perfume and tobacco breath. I lucked out today—Miss Norden has a substitute.

"O.K., keep them closed. I'm doing eyeliner now."

The eyeliner feels cool and wet.

"I'm an army brat," Whitney says. "I've moved eight times.

I forgot the first two moves, but I can remember living in New York, Texas, Florida, Maryland, California, and now North Carolina. My mom's an army nurse."

"I'm a faculty brat. I've lived here my whole life," I say. I've looked out the same window at the same oak tree every morning and every night for as long as I can remember.

"Getting to know people is the hardest part. You have to jump right in and do it quick. You have to check out what's cool to wear—because it's different in every town. You have to listen to the way people talk and imitate it. I'm good at accents. How's my North Carolina accent? 'Hey, y'all, we're fixin' to go to lunch.'"

I open my eyes. "Good." Her accent is fakey. Is that the way we sound to her?

"In New York you go to the shore, in Maryland you go 'down the ocean,' but here in North Carolina you go to the beach." She uses three vastly different accents, and I am impressed, even though she gives "beach" about three syllables. "You're looking good, girl. Now we need mascara." She rifles through a plastic, zippered cosmetics case. "Look at the ceiling."

I study the stippled tiles above my head. There is a large stain that I imagine is shaped like Atlantis. Whitney roughly strokes my lashes with the mascara wand.

"You have to know who the popular kids are and hang out with them. Get invited to all the parties."

The cosmetics make gentle clunking sounds as she shoves her hand in the case and moves it around, searching for a new brush or something. "But whenever I move, I always like to find someone I can really talk to." A soft brush strokes my cheeks. "O.K., now, pucker up."

I keep my eyes closed. Something cool and waxy slides over my pursed lips.

"You look fabulous. Go check yourself in the mirror."

I start to put my glasses back on.

"No, no, without the glasses," she says.

"I need them to climb down from the toilet," I say. God, what a dweeb.

I climb down, cross the bathroom, and peer at myself. I have to get about three inches from the mirror to see clearly. Whitney is looking over my shoulder, her face a hazy, unreadable white blob.

I look like. . . like a different person. Like someone who has lots of friends and goes to sleepover parties every weekend and gets phone calls and e-mail from boys.

"You have a nice heart-shaped face," says Whitney. "You should part your hair on the side, not in the middle. And don't wear your glasses all the time—just stick them on the top of your head in between classes, and only put them on when you need to see the board." Whitney props my glasses on top of my head. "There. Very glamorous."

"I better get back to language arts," I say. I'm feeling guilty, but fluttery and excited, too.

She digs into her back jeans pocket and pulls out two bent and flattened cigarettes. "Want one?"

I shake my head violently so that my glasses, perched on my head, wobble.

"Sure?"

I nod. She shrugs and climbs onto the sink to open the bathroom's one filthy window. A fall breeze swirls in. When she lights the cigarette, the match makes a loud, flaring sound, and I can hear the ends of the tobacco leaves sizzling.

"Thanks for the makeover," I say. "I better go."

"O.K., Carl." She blows out the match. "You look good, girl." No one has ever called me "Carl." She smiles at me and blows a thin blue smoke ring. It floats toward me, growing bigger and fatter like a doughnut. I think about the Cheshire Cat in *Alice in Wonderland*. "Call me tonight, O.K.?"

I duck out of the bathroom and hurry down the hall, my footsteps echoing. The doors of the classrooms and the rows of lockers are looming blurs on either side of me. The glasses on my head are wobbling, and I stop to straighten them. I yearn to put them back on so I can see, but I think about how I looked in the mirror in the bathroom, with the blush and the lip gloss and the eye makeup, and I don't.

I walk into the classroom. Everyone is reading. I return the hall pass to the substitute and slide behind my desk. Floating moonlike shapes that I know are faces turn toward me. Only two people's faces are close enough for me to see their expressions. Arlene and Zack.

Arlene's mouth is hanging so far open a small plane could fly in. She slaps her hand over it. But I don't care, because I think Zack is smiling. I can't explain it, but that makes me feel so good I swear I'll walk blind through the halls of this school for the rest of the year.

"MOM'S GOING TO MAKE you take off that makeup," says Matt on his way outside to shoot baskets. "You look like a clown."

He even follows Mom inside to gloat when she gets home from work, but he's disappointed. "Carly, guess what?" She waves a Manila envelope at me, which she says is a letter from a prestigious private university stating that my excellent grades and achievement scores have made me eligible to practice taking the SAT as a seventh grader. She's signed me up to take it in January. "This is really exciting! That way we can see the areas we need to work on, and you'll get plenty of practice before taking the real thing."

"The SAT?" I say.

"Yes, the Scholastic Aptitude Test. It's the most important test you'll ever take in your whole life. What you get on the SAT determines where you will go to college. It determines your entire future."

"College is seven years away." Some mascara has gotten in my eye, and I blink spastically.

"It's never too early to start thinking about it, sweetie.

Arlene has been invited to take the test, too," she adds, "so you two can go together."

"What's the highest possible score you can make on the SAT?" I ask.

"Sixteen hundred. Eight hundred on English, eight hundred on math."

"That's what Arlene will make," I say. I take a breath, and my chest feels tight.

"Carly, what in the world? Are you wearing makeup? Makeup is for older women. You have the natural beauty of youth. Now, go in the bathroom and wash it off."

THAT NIGHT I'M SUPPOSED to be writing a report on *The Outsiders,* but instead I call Whitney and tell her about Mom and the makeup.

"No problem. Meet me in the bathroom anytime you want, and I'll make you up. You can always wash it off before your mom sees you." She changes the subject. "Did you hear there's going to be a big party at Jeremy Gleason's house Friday night? I have to get invited. Are you going?"

"No," I say but immediately start wishing I were. Just talking on the phone for a few minutes with Whitney gives me a glimpse of this sparkling life I never knew existed.

"Well, if I get invited, I'll tell them to invite you, too," she says.

Whitney and I talk on the phone several nights that week. I feel as if I'm getting to know the popular people even though I've never spoken to them. She tells me about her mom's boyfriend, who is definitely rich because he drives a red sports car. He's going to marry her mom pretty soon, she says, and then she will move to a bigger house and have her own TV and stereo in her room.

On Friday I say hi to Whitney in the hall beside my locker and overhear her talking with some other girls about Jeremy Gleason's party.

"Did you get invited?" I ask when the other girls leave.

"Yeah!" she says. "It's tonight!"

"Oh." I don't say, "I wish I were invited," out loud, but I guess my face shows it.

Whitney claps a hand over her mouth. "Oh, Carly, I forgot about getting you an invitation. Sorry."

When Arlene asks me in language arts if I'm coming over to write, I say, "Sure." I go to Arlene's and try out Juliet's makeup while Arlene does most of the writing. I am thinking about the party I wasn't invited to and don't get my heart into the novel until halfway through the chapter. While we're writing, Arlene brings up the SAT. She says it's a great honor to be asked to take the SAT as a seventh grader, and she is going to start studying at Thanksgiving. "You should, too," she says.

I rub on some purple eye shadow and don't answer.

# chapter 8

# *The Magic*

TALAR MASSAGED HIS HAND while he reviewed the column of hieroglyphics he had just completed. Then he rolled his head from shoulder to shoulder to loosen his neck muscles. His back ached from being hunched in the same position for so many hours. He felt the tickle of a slight breeze, and the single candle beside his clay tablet flickered. The rain had finally stopped for the night. Outside the window, the moon's position in the sky showed it was very late. One of the sacred bulls out in the palace yard sighed loudly in his sleep.

Talar's time was up. He was supposed to report to Da by midnight, but he still had eighty years of history left to record. He'd found nothing written down. Worse, the princesses had disappeared, and the king had sent one hundred of his best men in search of them.

The other scribes thought he was nuts.

"Hey, what's with the overtime?" Ribalt, the scribe next to Talar, had joked as he laced his sandals in preparation for walking home that day. "Aren't you going to the chariot race? You're making the rest of us look bad."

Why *was* he doing this? What if the old wise man was off his rocker, the way everyone thought. What if Talar was wasting his time?

Ribalt finished lacing his sandals and stood up. "Well, happy scribbling, buddy."

THE MOON LIT HIS way as Talar climbed the steep, narrow stairs of the pyramid with the unfinished clay tablets in a satchel over his shoulder. They were incredibly heavy. It had never occurred to him that he'd have to be so strong to be a scribe. He would simply take the wise man his incomplete history and explain that he couldn't finish it. He counted the steps to make the climb easier. One hundred and forty-four.

At the top he leaned on his knees to catch his breath, then straightened and gasped at the incredible view. To the east he could see all the way to the ocean, where starlight glittered on the restless surface of the waves and the masts of Atlantis's many ships were lined at the docks. The towering volcano, with a dense veil of smoke encircling its peak, rose like a dark giant to the west.

The wise man sat upon a stone bench a few feet away from Talar, gazing at the stars. The thunder stone in Da's staff glowed faintly. Then, to Talar's amazement, a clay tablet and a stylus lifted from the surface of a stone table in the observatory, floated through the air, and hovered near Da's right hand. Da plucked the stylus from the air and made a drawing. The clay tablet remained suspended by Da's elbow.

"I've been waiting for you," said Da with a smile. A pillow floated from somewhere behind the wise man and settled near his feet. "Please sit down. Take the stylus, and I will tell you the rest of the history."

Talar gulped, speechless. He sat.

Da told Talar that one hundred years ago, people in Atlantis had not cared about the amount of land or number of goats they owned. They had been kind and generous to one another and to Poseidon and the other gods. When it came time, they gladly sacrificed their best corn, their best lambs, their best bulls. The kings before Avalach, all brothers, had lived in harmony with the others on the island. One hundred years ago, all of the people of Atlantis knew how to read and write. Now these skills were almost forgotten.

"You're right," agreed Talar. "The other scribes mostly keep records of the numbers of soldiers, ships, wheat fields, bulls, mines, and racehorses owned by the king. They're good with numbers but have forgotten the writing part. As the newest scribe, I was given the work of writing down the history. It's the least important thing, the king said."

"Yes, now they are foolish and greedy," said Da. "But in the old days the ten kings, originally all brothers and sons of Poseidon, met every five years. They donned azure robes and peacefully discussed the future of Atlantis. They wrote the laws of Atlantis on a tall copper pillar in the Temple of Poseidon. But now generations have passed, and years before you were born, King Avalach repudiated the other kings and had the pillar destroyed. The people don't show up for ceremonies anymore, and when they do come with sacrifices, they are worm-eaten and scrawny—the worst they can offer, not the best."

"King Avalach has been at war with the other kings ever since I can remember," said Talar.

Da nodded. "Today the people of Atlantis care only about acquiring more tunics, more jewels, more weapons. They do not care about the laws of the gods or about each other. They have no loyalty to the king. The only reason King Avalach has remained in power is because he possesses the ancient Mirror of the Oracle."

"What is that?"

"Legend has it that this magic mirror was made by the gods themselves. The mirror shows the truth about everyone who looks into it. King Avalach uses the mirror to learn the truth about his enemies. Once he knows, he can defeat them. If he should ever lose the power of that mirror, he could be defeated."

Da went on to say that he, too, years ago, had donned an azure robe and debated the future of Atlantis along with the kings. He had been revered as the only wise man who remembered why the pyramid had been built in the first place, who knew the legends of Atlantis all the way back to the beginning, and who could truly tell the future by the stars. He had seen his own laws inscribed on the Pillar of Orichalcum. He had seen his own face in the Mirror of the Oracle.

"How old are you?" asked Talar.

"That is a difficult question," said Da, staring at the stars. "At least eight hundred years."

"You're kidding. And why have you been alone at the top of the pyramid for so long?" Talar continued. "Why did the king and queen banish you after your warning about the destruction of Atlantis?"

"I did not agree with King Avalach's way of doing things and said so openly many times. King Avalach did not dare oppose me because I was the most powerful soothsayer. But then I made one single mistake. I predicted a drought . . . and instead we have had torrential rains. King Avalach now tells people that my wisdom has disappeared, that my magic powers are gone. And people believe him. I know that a great catastrophe is about to befall the people of Atlantis, or I would never have gone to see the king." Da stood. He seemed taller than Talar remembered. "Now that you are here, you might as well stay and help me prepare." Da lifted his staff high. The wide sleeves of his tunic swayed in the wind. "Look at the sky," he said.

Talar looked up.

WHEN LYDIA OPENED HER eyes, the trees outside the wall of the cave looked gray and filmy, and the songs of the birds seemed muffled by the softness of the morning air. Eva lay sleeping on the cave floor beside her, her kinked copper hair spread in the dirt. They had traveled yesterday to the ridge that the flying man pointed out to them and found this small cave when the afternoon rains came.

Queen Lannu had once told Lydia that she was born three minutes before Eva. Lydia reminded herself often that for three full minutes she'd been a leader, a bold pioneer. And then her sister had been born.

Lydia felt the slight weight of the small mirror in her pocket. She was still bothered by the fact that she couldn't see herself. She took out the mirror and held it in front of her face. Nothing—a smooth, blank surface. How infuriating that Eva could see herself but Lydia couldn't.

A pebble poked Lydia in the small of her back, and she shifted her weight as she slid the mirror back into her pocket. They had eaten nothing but a few berries yesterday. She was hungry. A sliver of the sun began to show over the horizon.

Eva was still fast asleep. The minute she woke up, she would have ideas about what to do today. For the moment it was nice to just lie here and make no plans.

Lydia thought of Leorbur and the silky feathers flying all around them when he crashed. His curly eyelashes, his flaming blue eyes. His arms, covered with golden fuzz that looked incredibly soft.

She *could* go visit him alone, before Eva woke up. She could leave a note saying, "Be right back." She'd never been anywhere without Eva, never been anywhere that wasn't Eva's idea, but really, why not? After all, next week she would be thirteen. Most Atlantean girls were married by then, or at least promised to the son of one of their father's friends or relatives.

She and Eva had been promised twice now, in fact. The first time they had been betrothed to the sons of two of the other Atlantean kings, but King Avalach had recently declared war on both of their fathers, so the engagements had been understandably called off. Both boys had terrible acne, and she and Eva had counted themselves lucky to be set free. And now they had been promised to Driz, the rain god. By comparison, acne didn't seem so bad.

The idea of visiting the flying man became more and more appealing, as if he were a magnet pulling her to him. He would probably have something to eat. If Lydia brought back food, Eva would admire her ingenuity. She scribbled Eva a note in the dirt with a stick and crawled out of the cave. She did not take the time to braid her hair as usual but left it flying wild like Eva's.

It was not easy to get Nya going. With a puzzled prick of her silver ears, the mare tried to turn back to look at Sphinx grazing a few yards away. The white edges of Nya's nervous eyes looked like new moons.

"You're not following Sphinx today," Lydia said. "I'm scared, too, but we can do it." She leaned over Nya's neck and urged her forward with a firm kick. Nya obeyed.

Nya climbed to the open area on top of the ridge before Lydia pushed her to a gallop. Lydia drew in the shockingly cold morning air, and her heart pumped wildly. Nya's nostrils steamed, and her hoofs were like drumbeats, and Lydia thought for a moment that the mare could be transforming into a dragon and any second take flight in a billow of fire and smoke.

A fine breeze threaded the grass on the plain below. Lydia searched the hilltops above the tree line for a large, clumsy bird.

She did not see one, but she did see a pear-shaped balloon the color of ivory rising slowly from a rocky ledge about ten stadia away. Someone seemed to be hanging onto lines attached to the bottom. The balloon, with its dangling cargo, lifted up and up and then drifted with the wind across the plain, like a floating jellyfish. Then it began to sink toward the tops of the scattered trees.

Was it? Could it be? Keeping the balloon in sight, Lydia galloped headlong through grass and thickets. She caught up with the balloon just in time to hear someone shout, "Arghhhh!" then hit the ground running, turn two somersaults, and sprawl into a pricker bush.

It was Leorbur, of course. When Lydia got to him, he was stuck in the bush and hopelessly tangled in the balloon lines. He had a cut lip and a red welt on his forehead.

"Hello," he said pleasantly. "It's you again. Where's your sister?"

"Um . . . still asleep, back in the cave."

"Oh." He smiled. "Could you, would you mind . . . I seem to be somewhat tangled up."

"Not at all," she said. Lydia felt her face get hot as she unwrapped the tangled hemp lines from his tan, fuzzed arms. Always up to this point in her life, Eva had been there to decide what to say and do. Now that she was on her own, Lydia had such a conflicting rush of fear, excitement, and nervousness that she felt lightheaded.

Finally she got him free and helped him stand. He brushed himself off.

"Thank you. Did you see much of the flight?" He began coiling up rope, talking rapidly. "Obviously it's quite uncomfortable for the pilot. A basket or a seat would be an improvement."

"Are you all right? You're awfully banged up," Lydia said.

"Oh, fine, fine, just a scratch here and there," he said with a blithe smile. He pulled the collapsed balloon into a heap. "I made it out of silk. Could you get that end? Fold toward me."

Lydia took one end of the balloon and carried it toward him as if in a formal dance. Their hands touched as the two ends of the balloon met. His eyes were inches away from hers, bright as blue marbles. He had a drop of blood at the corner of his mouth. Lydia tentatively reached up to wipe it away. He flinched like a startled bird but then let her rub off the blood with her thumb. "Uh . . . how did you get the balloon to rise?" she asked.

"I watched sparks floating in a fire and realized the smoke makes things rise. I got a small balloon to go up to a hundred feet before I made this big one." He folded the balloon again.

"That's amazing."

"You know, you're lighter than I am. I bet you or your sister would go higher." Leorbur hung the coiled hemp lines over his shoulders and slung the folded balloon over his back. "But I won't ask you to try it until we get a basket made. How are you at weaving?" He started off through the grass.

"Oh, pretty good." Lydia had not woven so much as a place mat in her life. The slaves did that. She trotted beside him, taking two steps to his one. She was amazed how easy it was to have an adventure without Eva.

Leorbur walked right by Nya, whose ears pricked forward, then in opposite directions as he passed. Leorbur stopped. "Is that your horse?" He actually looked at Lydia for the first time, the intensity of his stare seeming to bore right through her head.

"Yes, this is Nya."

"Can she carry the balloon and ropes?"

"Of course." Nya stamped her feet and snorted but accepted the load. Lydia stepped onto a rock and mounted her.

"I keep my supplies in a cave near where I took off." Leorbur strode toward the rocky ledge. "But first we should go get your sister."

Lydia sighed as she rode up beside him. She felt guilty for not thinking of Eva herself, and a little annoyed that he had. "Yes, we should, of course. Would you . . . do you want to ride?"

"Sure." They found a nearby tree stump, and Leorbur grasped her hand and pulled himself up and over Nya's flank. Lydia felt his warm breath by her ear. The damp heat of his thighs and chest behind her raised goose bumps from the nape of her neck to the small of her back.

"O.K., let's go," he said.

Lydia guided Nya back across the top of the ridge. The sun was up now and warm on her arms and face. Against her left shoulder she felt the steady beat of the flying man's heart. She composed in her mind what she would say to Eva, how she would explain. Straining under the extra load, Nya picked her way down the rocky embankment, and Lydia ducked her head into the shadowed cave, calling her sister's name. Eva was nowhere to be seen.

Curiously, Leorbur seemed nearly as upset as she was.

# chapter 9

## *Something Happens Between Me and Arlene*

I HAVE BEEN WAITING for a chance to meet Whitney in the bathroom for another makeover, and a couple of weeks later that chance finally comes. Miss Norden has a substitute again. I tell the substitute I have to leave class because I'm trying out for the seventh-grade play, *You're a Good Man, Charlie Brown.* The substitute doesn't know that the tryouts are really after school. Obviously, Arlene would attend any actual tryouts. She wants to be Lucy, because her father has said it's the most interesting part.

A few minutes later, Whitney and I are standing on the toilet again, and she is rubbing stuff on my face and telling me how everyone played this game called Truth or Dare at Jeremy Gleason's party. Someone dared her to run around Jeremy's backyard with her bra over her shirt backward, and she did.

When she is finished, I look in the mirror and see she has put green eye shadow on me. "That looks good," I say. I look like a mermaid.

"Keep the eye shadow," she says, smiling, and presses the frosted cylinder into my hand.

On the bus the next day I put on some eye shadow and stick my glasses on top of my head. Without my glasses, everybody is a blob until I get about ten feet away, so at lunch I almost walk right by the table where Whitney is sitting. I notice there's an empty seat next to her.

"I'm having a sleepover tonight," Whitney is saying, just as I sit down. "Tell your mom to bring you at about six."

"A sleepover?" I ask. I put on my glasses. I'm not sure if she was talking to me or a girl across the table with streaked blond hair.

"Yeah," says Whitney after a minute. "We're having pizza."

A sleepover! I smile broadly at Zack Wingo, who happens to be sitting at the next table with some guys from the cross-country team. He smiles back, and Brett Hunsucker, sitting next to him, sees and pokes his arm teasingly. Zack blows the paper off his straw right into Brett's face, and then Brett lobs an empty milk carton at Zack's ear. Zack ducks, glancing in our direction. I look away and feel myself blushing.

"Oooh, do you think he's cute?" Whitney is one of those people who tears things into little pieces if she doesn't want to eat them, and she's doing that to her hamburger roll.

"Who?" I look at her, wide-eyed, and fake innocence.

"Zack Wingo. The cross-country guy from California who draws cartoons."

I don't answer, but my face gets hot. She smiles at the blond girl and pops a grape into her mouth. I look down at my tray and realize for the first time that the little bowl of what I thought was mashed potatoes is actually cauliflower.

AFTER LUNCH A TALL, fuzzy person with long arms waving comes toward me in the hall, and I realize it's Arlene. I'm supposed to go to her house and write with her again tonight. I get a stomach cramp when I think about trying to explain the sleepover at Whitney's, so I duck into a side hallway when she walks by.

I make sure I get to language arts right as the bell rings so Arlene and I won't have time to talk, but she quickly passes me a note. I open it and pull down my glasses.

"My audition was great! I really, really hope I got Lucy!" it says. I had forgotten all about the tryouts for *You're a Good Man, Charlie Brown.* I scribble, "Great!" and send the note back and then pretend to be concentrating on Miss Norden's every word.

She assigns us the next three chapters of *The Outsiders* and hands out questions to answer. Marty Bellows raises his hand and says, "Is this for a grade?" Miss Norden sighs and says yes.

Arlene and I usually walk to the buses together, and I'm sure she will bring up tonight, but it so happens that Miss Norden calls me up to her desk after class. I wave Arlene on, saying, "I'll talk to you later."

"I understand you missed most of class yesterday to go to tryouts for *You're a Good Man, Charlie Brown,*" Miss Norden says. I'd been so relieved about Arlene that she has caught me completely off guard. The lines on her forehead are deep, and her intense green eyes behind her glasses pin me like a butterfly to a corkboard.

My heart freezes. I swallow. I decide the best thing to say is nothing.

"So what part did you get, Carly?" she presses me.

"Um, I didn't get a part," I mumble.

"That must be," she says, "because you didn't go to the auditions, which, as we all know, were *after* school. I was there. I'm directing the play. That's why I had a substitute— I was getting ready for the auditions."

I hang my head. I review possible things to say, and my best choice seems to be silence.

"But you're in luck," she continues. "So many seventh graders wanted to try out that we've extended auditions to this afternoon as well. I'd like you to come."

"I get really bad stage fright." I have a flash memory of the time Mom signed me up for the children's choir at church. The choir director told Mom I had perfect pitch during rehearsals. But the first time I stood in front of the congregation and opened my mouth, no sound whatsoever came out, not even a squeak. Mom said she sat in the pew and cried for me because even my eyeballs were shaking.

Miss Norden hands me my first *Outsiders* report. In the top corner she has written, "I know you can do better than this! C+." She comes around the desk, leans against it, and crosses her arms. "You have the potential to be an excellent student, Carly. You're reading on a high-school level, and your writing skills are exceptional." She cocks her head. "But somehow I get the feeling that you're not really applying yourself."

"Yes, I am," I say.

"You know," she says, "a lot of smart girls get sidetracked in middle school, and it takes them a long time to get back on course. Some girls never do. I think you deserve another chance. I'm not going to send you to after-school detention for skipping class this time, and I won't put it on your permanent record . . . if you'll try out for *You're a Good Man, Charlie Brown.*"

"I get stage fright," I say again. "Really, really bad." Just thinking about it makes me feel nauseous.

"You'll get over it." Miss Norden squeezes my arm and smiles at me. Maybe she thinks she's being some kind of hero, but I think she's the wickedest person I've ever known. I'm glad I'm not her pet. I hate her. Totally.

I CALL DAD AT work because he has a light schedule on Fridays. I tell him I have to stay after school to try out for the play.

"Try out for the play?" he says. "Well, great. I'm pleased to hear that."

I can't exactly tell him that Miss Norden is making me try out because I skipped class. "I probably won't get a part," I add. In fact, I plan for my audition to be extremely bad.

"No, that's great, Carly," he says. "You're so good when you and Arlene do your skits together, it's about time you came out of your shell and tried something like that. I'm very proud of you."

"You are?" I say.

"You bet. I'll be there to pick you up at five, then."

There are probably thirty kids in the gym waiting to audition. I scan the bleachers for someone to sit with. Since

Arlene tried out yesterday, she isn't here. My mouth feels dry. Miss Norden sits on the front bleacher with stacks of audition sheets. Kids are telling her which parts they want to try out for, and she gives them a sheet for each character. Groups of kids are sitting on the bleachers reading scenes together.

Suddenly I spot Zack Wingo and Marty Bellows. They're reading a scene. I stand and watch. Zack is reading the part of Schroeder, and he must have taken acting lessons in California. He's really good.

Miss Norden sees me. "Have you decided which part you'd like to try for, Carly?"

"No."

She hands me two sheets. "The major female roles are Lucy and Charlie Brown's younger sister, Sally," she says. "And then we'll need lots of good singers for the chorus."

I sit by myself and reconsider my plan to have a really, really bad audition. If Zack gets a part, I would get to be around him every afternoon for more than a month.

The audition is in a little room beside the stage. Miss Norden and another teacher, who looks friendly and encouraging, sit behind student desks. They ask me to sing any song I know, and all I can think of is a song from *Oliver!* that I used to sing with Arlene. I get off to a bad start, then turn red and stop, beginning to feel dizzy and sick. The roaring starts again in my ears, and all I want is to get out of the room.

"It's O.K., take all the time you need," Miss Norden says gently. "I used to be afraid to get up in front of the classroom . . . but I did it. So I know you can, too. Take a slow, deep breath."

I inhale deeply, closing my eyes. I open my eyes and let my breath out slowly. Miss Norden has such a kind smile on her face, I want to cry. I start out singing so softly, I'm sure they can't hear me, and I want to get it over with, so I'm singing really fast, too.

Somysongcomesoutlikethis,alljumbledtogetheranditlastsmaybeoneminutetotal.

I can't exactly remember what happens after that. I think I read a scene where I play Sally, or maybe it's Lucy. I just remember Miss Norden saying, "Thanks, Carly, you did a good job. I know it wasn't easy for you. We'll post the cast on the front door by the office after seven tonight, if you want to stop by."

I barely make it out of the room before my knees buckle and I slide down the wall just outside the door. I sit there watching my kneecaps shake while two more people go in and come back out.

Afterward, when I climb into Dad's car, he pats my arm. "How'd it go?"

"I'm pretty sure I didn't get a part," I say. I hold my hand out to see if it's stopped shaking yet. It hasn't, so I jam it under my thigh.

"Well, however it turns out, I'm proud of you for trying," he says. I don't answer, because I'm sure he wouldn't be proud if he knew why I auditioned. Dad drops me off at home and leaves to close up his office. When I get inside the house, the phone's ringing.

"So what did Miss Norden want to talk to you about? And when are you coming over?" It's Arlene.

"Uh, let's see," I say. "I don't know if I can come tonight. Mom has to work on her grant proposal, so I don't have a ride." I'm trying to figure out a way I can go to Whitney's sleepover.

"Ride your bike," says Arlene quickly. "Or Dad will come get you."

"Well, I'm not feeling too good," I say. "I might be getting sick."

"Oh." Arlene's voice changes. Now she can tell I don't want to come over, and she doesn't know how to act since it's never happened before. I don't know how to act, either. I suddenly think with regret about the navy-blue ceiling with the stars. I can just see Arlene, doing that stupid scissors exercise with her long, skinny legs. "O.K., well." There is a long silence.

Part of me misses Arlene already and feels sorry for Eva and Lydia, frozen on the page, waiting for us to show up tonight. "Well," Arlene says, "maybe I'll just write some by myself."

"By yourself?" That's not fair. I don't want to go over there, but I don't want her to write anything by herself, either.

"Yeah. Actually, I know." Her voice warms again with her idea. "I'll write a chapter and e-mail it to you."

"But," I say, stalling, "we didn't really decide whether they're going to fall in love or have an adventure."

"No love," says Arlene. "I've decided I want it to be two girls on a quest."

"But in *Sense and Sensibility* Elinor falls in love with Edward. In *These Happy Golden Years* Laura Ingalls falls in love with Almanzo Wilder. In *Little Women* Laurie falls in love with Jo," I argue. "Someone falls in love in every really good book."

"But I don't want them to fall in love. Boys get to go on quests all the time. I want our girl characters to go on one for a change. Besides, I don't know how to write about love." Suddenly Arlene's voice sounds forlorn, and I feel guilty. She's right. I always write the romantic stuff.

"A quest for what?" I say.

"To discover the secret of the mirror, of course."

The secret of the mirror. I feel so torn. I'm dying to go to Whitney's. At the same time, the round and ancient image of the Mirror of the Oracle flashes alluringly in my imagination. "Let me see if Mom will let me come. I'll call you back."

I punch in Mom's work number. I decide I will ask her about going to Whitney's first. If she says no, I'll ask about spending the night with Arlene.

When she answers the phone, I say, "Mom, I've been invited to a sleepover at Whitney's house."

As soon as I hear her voice, I realize I've lucked into one of those incredibly rare situations—she is too busy to care *what* I do as long as she doesn't have to drive me. I can hear her tapping away at the keyboard, working on her grant proposal as she talks. "And her parents are definitely going to be there?"

"Yes."

"And they've said it's all right for you to come?"

"Yes, yes . . ."

"And you'll only watch PG-13, no R's, and no horror?"

"Yes, yes." I'm hopping from one foot to the other.

"Well, I've got to finish this thing; it has to be postmarked by tonight. Dad will have to take you on the way to Matt's soccer practice."

"O.K."

"And be sure to give him the number."

"O.K., O.K."

She hesitates. "Don't you usually write with Arlene on Friday nights?"

"Yeah, but not tonight."

There is a long moment of silence before she answers. "Well, have a good time, sweetie."

"O.K., I will."

"And, Carly—"

"What?" I'm ready to explode with impatience.

"Use good judgment."

"O.K., O.K., bye!"

Whoopee! I turn a cartwheel down the hall, then call Whitney and get directions to her house. I open my dresser drawers and pull out clothes as if I were a human tornado— shirts and jeans and pajamas—and hurl them onto the bed. I toss my favorite stuffed bunny on top. I forget all about calling Arlene back.

WHITNEY LIVES IN A white clapboard house with green shutters in a neighborhood halfway between my house and the school. There is a swing on the porch and a pot of bright pink, fluffy flowers on the front step. Dad pulls into the driveway. He turns off National Public Radio, which is the only station he listens to. All they do on that station is talk. About the stock market or rain forests or faraway countries like Indonesia. It is so boring.

Matt has been bouncing his soccer ball on the back of my seat the whole way over.

"Hey, dingleberry, hurry up. I'm going to be late for soccer."

"Stop calling me that! And stop bouncing that ball off my seat!"

"Kids, quiet. Is this it, Carly? Do you have a house number?" Dad looks at my scribbled directions. The only place I've ever spent the night, besides home or my grandparents', is Arlene's. This feels weird. A curtain moves, and I see Whitney peering out a window. When her face disappears, I know she's coming to the door.

"This is it. That's Whitney." My fears melt away, and I grab my sleeping bag and overnight bag and jump out of the car. The front door opens, and Whitney steps onto the porch.

Dad gets out of the car with a hesitant smile. "Hi, Whitney. I'm Carly's dad."

Whitney doesn't smile at him, and I can barely hear her when she says, "Hi." This is weird because Arlene tells my parents everything and hangs around in the kitchen acting out scenes as long as they will pay attention. Sometimes Mom or Dad will finally say, "Carly, why don't you take Arlene back to your room?" to get rid of her.

"Thanks for having Carly over." Dad puts his arm around my shoulder. "I should find out from your mom what time to pick her up in the morning."

"Mom said to say we'll call," says Whitney quickly. "Hurry up, Carly." She grabs my sleeping bag. "We're calling the radio station to request songs."

"Does your mom have a minute to come out and talk right now?" Dad has worry lines around his eyes.

"Well, she can't. She's in the shower."

"Oh." Dad looks embarrassed. He glances at his watch.

"Dad!" Matt calls from the backseat. "C'mon, we're going to be late."

Dad's arm tightens around my shoulder. "O.K., sweetie, have fun. And listen, as soon as Matt's game is over, I'll be home, so if you get a stomachache or anything, just give us a call."

This is code. Mom and Dad and I have always had this agreement that if I go somewhere, anywhere, and things aren't going well, I can call home and say I have a stomachache, and they'll come and get me right away. Dad brushes his lips across my forehead and squeezes my shoulder once more before he moves toward the car. The warmth of his body is suddenly gone.

Whitney drags me inside, but I turn to look at Dad through the screen door. He is backing the car out, watching behind him, and the only person I can see is Matt, who mouths the word *dingleberry* and pulls his face into a horrible grimace. I feel bad, because Whitney was sort of rude to Dad. I hope Whitney's mom doesn't yell a lot.

"So your mom's in the shower?" I say as we start through the family room, a narrow space with blue furniture and a beige carpet. I don't hear the shower going.

"No, she's at work." Whitney grins and raises her eyebrows. "She's a nurse, remember? Her shift is over at ten." My throat goes dry. Whitney lied to my dad. Slowly I follow her through the kitchen and dining room. She's wearing flared jeans with a peace symbol ironed onto one back pocket and a yin-yang ironed onto the other. "Ashley and Tracy are here," she says.

I try to place them. I think Juliet said once that Tracy French-kissed Craig Weisener four times at the pool this summer. I follow Whitney into her room, where seated on the bed I see the girl with streaked blond hair who sat across from us at lunch today. That must be Tracy. The other girl, Ashley, is big-boned with a wide face and straight brown hair to her waist. She's the same person who did the imitation of me that day when Whitney made fun of Arlene. Smoke clouds curl around their heads like layers of gray gauze. Whitney has rock-band posters plastered on the walls and a light that turns everything in the room purple. She has a lava lamp and her own telephone, sleek and black.

I look out the window. Dad's car is already gone.

As we walk in, Ashley slams the telephone down and starts laughing. "I just called up this person and told them they had won the Wonderbra Sweepstakes and their prize was a size forty-four double D." Ashley and Tracy roll around on the bed. They can't stop laughing.

Who did they call, I wonder. Just a number from the phone book?

The phone rings. Whitney drops my sleeping bag on the floor and grabs the receiver. "Babes Central." She listens for a minute, then her eyes go wide, and she smiles. "O.K. See you then." She jumps up on the bed and screams. "They're coming!" Tracy claps her hand to her mouth.

"Who's coming?" I ask.

"The boys!" All three of them clasp hands and jump on the bed.

"What boys?" I stand holding my pink overnight bag with my name in pastel letters on the side. The stuffed bunny was definitely a mistake.

"Craig Weisener, Marty Bellows, and Zack Wingo!"

All three of them squeal again. I sit down on the edge of the bed and hug my overnight bag. I get this tingly feeling as if all the nerves in my body just snapped to attention, shouting, "Red alert!" A wave of hot saliva washes up my throat as I try to remember if I told Whitney that I like Zack.

"We all need makeovers before they get here!" Whitney announces.

"Me first!" says Tracy.

# chapter 10

## *When It Gets Dark*

WE ARE ALL FOUR made up with glitter on our cheeks and gel in our hair, sitting under the porch light. My glasses are on my head. A few minutes ago I heard Ashley ask Whitney, in a loud whisper, why she invited me. I didn't hear what Whitney said back. Right now the other three girls are arguing about whether a line in a song on the radio is "You can boogie with me anytime" or "You buy burgers for me with a dime."

"Or maybe it's 'You eat boogers with me in the slime,'" says Ashley.

"Gross!" Whitney and Tracy make gagging sounds.

"I don't know," says Ashley, giggling. "That's just what it sounds to me like they're saying."

It's not cold out; in fact, it's a warm autumn night, but I'm shaking. Whitney's mother hasn't come home.

I'm hungry. No one's mentioned the pizza, and I'm afraid to bring it up. I think about a dinner I had at Arlene's. Arlene and Juliet had made straight A's, and their parents, in honor of the occasion, served a dinner of extremely weird food that all started with A's. We had an artichoke-and-avocado dip for the appetizer. Then we had antipasto, which is an Italian salad with bologna and olives in it, and cream-of-asparagus soup. The main course was abalone fritters, made from a kind of shellfish, Arlene's mom said. Dessert was apple pie à la mode, which I had two slices of since I hadn't eaten too much of the other stuff.

I'm catapulted back to the present by the whir of bicycles and three tall shadows gliding toward us in the dark.

"Hey, there." Whitney stands up. The end of her cigarette glows. Ashley and Tracy stand behind her, giggling. I sit in a pool of shadow and don't move except to pull my glasses down so I can see.

The bikes squeal to a halt one by one, in a line, and the boys' Nikes scrape the asphalt. They could be cowboys on horseback. Any minute, I think, they will tip their hats and say, "Howdy, ma'am."

Craig Weisener speaks first. Craig Weisener of the four French kisses at the pool this summer. Craig Weisener, who always loses his bathing suit after a one and a half so all the girls know, firsthand, that he has nice buns. Craig Weisener, whose dad is the mayor. "What's up?" he says.

"Oh, nothin'." Whitney takes a drag of her cigarette and blows a smoke ring, like a fat lariat meant to loop around the boys' necks and drag them toward her.

Marty Bellows's legs are too short for him to keep sitting on his bike, so he gets off, trying to act real cool. "How ya doin'?" he says. Whitney told me Marty has a pool table and a Nintendo in his basement, and that's why the other guys let him hang out with them. He's the only one wearing a bicycle helmet.

Zack doesn't say anything. His wavy, dark hair gleams under the porch light. He's wearing a faded T-shirt, jeans, and his running shoes. His eyes look like a hawk's, dark and wary. He squints at me, trying to figure out who I am, I think.

"Do your parents know you're here?" Tracy leans with both hands on Craig's handlebars.

"Nah." Craig adjusts his baseball cap, which he is wearing backward. "We're all supposed to be spending the night in Marty's basement. We left the music on and stuffed towels in our sleeping bags in case his mom comes down."

Tracy giggles. "I can't believe y'all did that."

"Is your mom home?" Craig asks Whitney.

She shakes her head. "She gets off work at ten. She won't be home till ten-thirty."

"Plenty of time to go for a swim," Craig says.

Whitney turns to the rest of us. "Oooh, want to?"

"The pool's closed," I say.

Everybody stares at me.

"Duh," says Ashley.

"That would be affirmative, the pool *is* closed," says Craig.

I want to die, absolutely die. It's suddenly obvious to me, and I don't know why it wasn't before, that there are three boys and four girls.

"Well, Carly," says Whitney, "if you don't want to get in trouble, you can stay here and call the pool's phone number to warn us if my mom gets home early."

Everybody glares at me. I glare back. No, I don't want to get in trouble. But I don't want Zack to think I'm a chicken, and I don't want to be left here by myself, either. I could call Dad and say I have a stomachache. He would be here in ten minutes to get me, I know. I glance at Zack and swallow.

"I'll go," I say.

THE OTHER GIRLS RIDE double on the boys' bikes, their arms around the guys' waists and their legs flying out to the sides, like wings. I follow on Whitney's bike, which is too big for me. Whitney rides with Zack, and Tracy rides with Craig. Ashley gave the other two girls a dirty look when they stuck her with Marty Bellows. I guess she figured it was better than riding by herself, though, because she's riding with him, although she's about twice his size, and they finally end up stopping and switching places.

It's a bright, starry night, and the sliver of moon hangs like an orange peel in the sky, and our voices sound tinny and seem to get sucked into the warm, dark air. We have left Whitney's neighborhood, and we're in a nicer one. As I glide past a streetlight, I can see a brick house with columns and rows of bushes with white flowers. We turn onto an older street, and oak trees arch over us, muffling our voices with the silvery swish of their leaves in the night breeze. It's like the rest of the world is glued in one spot, and we're in a flashy bubble of excitement, passing everyone by.

The air feels silky but electric, and I think maybe on the way back, I will ride with Zack, and we will be like Lydia and the flying man galloping together across the plains of Atlantis, bareback on her horse, Nya. I try not to think about Whitney doubling with Zack right now. Of course Tracy was going to ride with Craig because of the French kisses, and Whitney is too cool and pretty to go with Marty. Riding double on a bike doesn't really mean anything.

The pool is in a cul-de-sac at the bottom of a hill.

"Whoooo!" We sweep down the hill, screaming, our hands high in the air. The wind forces streams of hot tears from the corners of my eyes, which streak across my temples and melt in my hair. My heart pumps like a giant piston, racking my entire chest like those cartoon characters whose hearts leap free of their bodies and beat in midair. I feel slightly nauseated, maybe from nervousness and hunger. As I brake to a stop, the smell of chlorine tickles the inside of my nose. We walk the bikes around to the back of the pool house so they can't be seen from the street.

Under the streetlights the pool glints like a silver mirror. The metal fence squeaks as Zack's and Whitney's silhouettes climb, arch over the top, then drop onto the concrete on the other side.

"Come on!" Their voices hiss with urgency. Soft splashes follow, and the pool's surface breaks into a million pieces.

"Oooh, it's warm," breathes Whitney.

The others climb and jump, except for Marty, who sits on top of the fence for a minute and presses a button that lights up his watch. I see a strobe of his thin face, green and eerie for a second, then it goes dark again.

"I don't know if my watch is waterproof." His voice sounds high and doubtful. He lowers himself carefully over the other side and hangs from both arms for several seconds before he lets go and slides down the fence.

What a dingleberry. Last time Miss Norden gave us chapters to read, Marty raised his hand, as usual, and said, "Is this for a grade?" And Miss Norden looked at the ceiling and breathed heavily for a minute, and then said between clenched teeth, "Yes, Marty, *everything* in this class is for a grade!"

I grab the iron mesh in both hands and start to pull myself up, shoving the toes of my shoes into the diamond-shaped fence holes. The fence squeals as if it's in pain.

By the time I drop to the cement inside the fence, everybody else is in the pool. Sometimes there are pool parties at night, and they turn on these cool underwater lights that make us look like we have greenish white frog skin. But they aren't on tonight, and it's mysterious, because I can hear the voices and splashes, but the dark, shiny ripples in the water could be dolphins or sharks.

I sit on the side and put my feet in. The water's warm. I try to make out the figures in the pool and see Marty's watch light up down at the shallow end.

Ashley is on the diving board, bouncing and singing, pretending she's holding a microphone. Her jeans, soaking wet, look like they weigh a hundred pounds, and I can see the outline of her bra through her wet T-shirt. She reaches the end of a song, throws her arms out like a diva, and jumps off the board.

Two people are in a dark corner of the deep end with their arms wrapped around each other like octopus tentacles. I know it's Tracy and Craig. It has to be.

And then I see Whitney and Zack sitting on the side, across the pool, and he holds out his arm with the tender white part facing up, and she walks her fingertips up the inside. His eyes are closed. I know this game. He's supposed to say, "Now," when he thinks she's gotten to his elbow.

"Now," he says and opens his eyes. He looks at her fingertips, poised on his arm.

"I didn't go all the way," says Whitney. "Ha-ha." Her ears do not stick out; they are snuggled close to her head, with gold hoops dangling, and her hair is wet and slick like a seal's.

He laughs, sounding embarrassed. He sees me on the other side of the pool. And then she shoves him in. Just boom, splash dunk, and she's laughing. And then it's really weird because he swims all the way across underwater. He doesn't come up until he gets to the edge. He holds on with one hand, breathing hard, treading water. His hand is four inches from mine.

"Aren't you going to get in?"

"Sure." I look down at the edges of my jeans, barely wet. I can hardly breathe.

"It looks like we might be in the play together," he adds. "I got Schroeder—you know, the kid who plays the piano."

Fireworks light the sky behind my eyes.

"I got a part?" My voice is a high squeak.

"I'm sure I saw your name in the chorus," he says. "So, yeah, you're in the play."

He acts as if he's going to stay and talk but then changes his mind. He pushes off and does the butterfly back across the pool. We'll have to stay after school together. A minute slides by, and I hardly dare to breathe.

Suddenly I remember Arlene. "Hey, Zack, did Arlene get a part?"

"Yeah," he says as he glides to the edge. "Lucy."

Of course. Lucy charges five cents for advice. Lucy is always going up to Charlie Brown and saying, "You blockhead!" Lucy is crazy about Schroeder. Arlene is going to have lots and lots of scenes with Zack.

Ashley is back on the board, pretending she is a diva again. Marty must have decided his watch is waterproof after all, because he's sitting cross-legged on the bottom in the shallow end and lighting up the watch and waving his arm around. I think of those deepwater fish that carry their own tiny lanterns, like glowing green pearls. Tracy and Craig have gotten out of the pool and moved to one of the lounge chairs. They don't seem to care who watches them.

I fold my glasses on the side of the pool, then let myself fall in. The water is so warm, my body feels more a part of it than the air. My clothes billow around me, making me feel as if I'm moving in slow motion. I swim toward the blobs that I know are Whitney and Zack.

Suddenly headlights crest the top of the hill. Between the chlorine and the loss of my glasses, the lights seem like supernovas.

"Car!" shouts Zack. Everybody scrambles out. We run for the darkest corner of the fence and climb over, gasping and dripping. By the time the car pulls up, we are huddled behind the pool house.

"The cops," whispers Zack. We plaster ourselves against the wall and try to control the chattering of our teeth as two police officers, one man and one woman, get out of the squad car and shine flashlights around the empty lawn chairs. We watch, holding our breath, as the two columns of light dance over the telltale wavelets and the diving board, still trembling. One flashlight beam comes to rest on my glasses, still folded neatly on the side of the pool.

# chapter 11

# *Caught*

I LIE ON MY bed and stare at the plain vanilla ceiling of my room. Maybe I should put up some stars. I could also spend some time putting up a dartboard. With Miss Norden's and Mom's and Dad's and the two police officers' faces on it. Nobody understands that all this stuff just happened to me, and there was nothing I could do to stop it.

My eyes wander to my closet. Until only recently I believed if I slid open the small, wooden door in the back corner, it would reveal an ancient tunnel with damp stone steps leading down, down—straight to an underground lake where I would come face to face, over a flickering candle, with none other than the disguised crown prince of the merpeople. He would greet me with great relief as the long-lost mermaid princess who is the only hope for his ailing and secret colony.

Now I know that what's really inside that little door is the handle Dad uses to shut off the water in this part of the house.

Outside the window is the oak tree that has been there my whole life. The leaves rustle like fairy wings in the breeze and throw flitting shadows around the walls of my room. A squirrel sits on his haunches and bares his yellow teeth at me. He throws an acorn, and it pings against the screen.

*You really acted very impulsively,* I imagine the stor book Emma to say.

*You should feel grateful that you were only gro for a month,* says Pollyanna.

*You must escape,* says Cleopatra.

I can't go anywhere except school, not eve

am allowed, oh joy, to attend the next meeting of the Young Scientists Club. Oh, and play practice, which starts in a week. Mom loves Miss Norden now; they are best friends. They had a long, chatty conversation on the phone, and they've had a meeting of the minds, I guess, on how great it will be for me to be in the play. I guess I feel differently about it myself now that I know Zack Wingo is playing Schroeder.

I see Keesey's shadow outside the window and pop the screen to let her in. She jumps onto my bed, tracking in a dead oak leaf and a few pine needles, then curls up by my pillow, making herself right at home.

BY SUNDAY AFTERNOON I haven't heard from Whitney, so I call her to see if she got in trouble. She says she is on the other line and will call me back, but I wait an hour, and she doesn't. I call Arlene to tell her what happened, but she says she already knows about it—that her parents were talking about how some juvenile delinquents got caught by the cops breaking into the pool on Friday night and how they went skinny-dipping, and that one of them was a professor's kid.

"We weren't skinny-dipping," I say. "We had our clothes on."

"Why would you do that?" she says, puzzled. "Didn't you know you'd get in trouble? It was so embarrassing to find out that the professor's kid was *you.*"

"I don't know, everybody else was doing it." I loop my finger through about four curls of the phone cord. Arlene sounds like my mother.

"And you were supposed to spend the night with me, anyway. You didn't even call me back."

"Sorry."

"And none of those girls are even in any advanced classes. Craig Weisener, even though his dad is the mayor, is practically in *remedial* reading. Why would you want to hang around with them?"

I try not to think about the time Whitney and Ashley

imitated Arlene and me walking down the hall at school, but it pops into my head, and I can't get it out. I feel my face grow hot. Why *do* I want to hang around with them? Arlene is supposedly my best friend. Only a month ago I prayed every night to be in her family and live at her house.

"I feel like I'm being interrogated by the White Witch or something." I mean the White Witch from *The Lion, the Witch and the Wardrobe.* The very evil White Witch.

"Yeah, well, maybe I should just call you Edmund." Arlene's voice takes on an edge. Edmund, the greedy brother who betrayed them all.

"I have to go," I say.

"Fine. I e-mailed you a chapter on Friday night, just like I said I would."

"You wrote a whole chapter?"

"Yeah."

So she really did write without me. A whole chapter by just Arlene.

I take a quick, shallow breath. "Well, O.K. I guess I'll read it."

"Fine. It's a quest. No love."

We are silent. I can hear Arlene breathing. She's probably doing some yoga pose.

"I thought you had to go," she finally says.

"I do."

"O.K. Bye."

Before I can hang up, there is a dial tone. I let myself fall back on the bed. I feel so terrible. There is no one on my side.

Mom isn't even speaking to me. She just looks at me and shakes her head in disbelief. Whenever I walk by Matt, he shapes the word *dingleberry* silently with his lips as he makes a small diving motion with his hands. I'd like to cover him with snail slime.

Being in the backseat of the police car was not something I

am going to forget anytime soon. There was wire mesh between the backseat and the front seat so I felt as if I were in a cage. It smelled like stale, greasy French fries and sweat. All four of us girls were squished into the backseat, wet thigh up against wet thigh. I got goose bumps when I thought about how I was sitting on the same seats CRIMINALS sit on every day. One of the police officers made a call on the radio to ask for backup. While we waited, Craig took his hat off and put it back on, again and again, and Marty paced back and forth, muttering, "Oh, man. GEEZ. Oh, man. GEEZ." Zack stood quietly with his arms crossed, staring first at his Nikes, then up at the black, lacy treetops. Within five minutes another police car appeared, and the cops ushered the boys into the backseat of that one. The sirens weren't on, but the blue lights swept around and around the trees, pool, and tennis courts like strobes from a UFO.

Tracy was wedged next to me, and her wet, blond hair dripped down my arm.

The policewoman's name was written on her nametag, but I couldn't read it. There was a dark bulge at her side, which I figured was a gun. She was tall with short, red hair and a square face, a square body. She did most of the talking while the other officer, whose name I also couldn't read, did the writing.

"How old are you?"

Ashley and I whispered twelve; Tracy and Whitney said thirteen. My teeth were chattering so hard, I bit my tongue.

"You realize, don't you, that if you were sixteen, you'd be arrested and thrown in jail for breaking and entering?"

"No, ma'am." It came out all raggedy, in four scared voices. Then Tracy started to sob.

"What are you going to do to us? My parents are going to kill me. I mean kill me. Please don't tell my parents."

The car engine came to life with an exceptionally loud roar as the male police officer turned the key in the ignition.

Then it came to me why I couldn't read the nametags: I didn't have on my glasses.

"Wait," I said with sudden panic. "I forgot my glasses. They're still on the side of the pool."

The driver turned in his seat to stare at me with what I'm sure must have been disgust. He called to the other police car. "Hey, Butch, one of these little girls left her glasses by the pool. Somebody needs to go get them."

"I will," said a voice, and Zack emerged from the backseat of the other cop car. The blue lights crisscrossed his back as he jogged to the fence in a lazy cross-country lope. We all watched in silence as he seemed almost to pole-vault over the fence, then took two steps and picked up my folded frames. A moment later he thrust them through the back window.

"Thanks," I breathed. His face came into sharp focus as I slid my glasses on. If I had eyelashes as long as his, they'd knock my glasses off. He had a freckle on his upper lip.

"No problem." He raised his hand in a half wave.

The rear door slammed, and the other squad car pulled away.

One by one, they took us home. None of us dared to talk. They tried to take Whitney first, but her mother was still at work, so we went to Tracy's. She lived in the nice neighborhood we'd ridden through on our bikes, in a large, brick house with a circular driveway. I watched in horror as the door opened, a golden rectangle in the darkness, and Tracy's mom's hand flew to her mouth as she saw her daughter standing there with a police officer. I could almost hear her gasp. Tracy went inside hanging her head. The door shut.

I was next. As we walked up my sidewalk, my soaked underwear was riding up, and the wet jeans were starting to chap my thighs.

"What you kids did was not only illegal, it was dangerous. Someone could have drowned." The officer held me loosely by the elbow. I wanted to rip my arm from her grasp but opted instead to pull away one tiny millimeter at a time.

We reached the front door. She rang the bell. Standing under the porch light, I saw that her nametag said Officer Mary Jo Snelling.

In church when we're supposed to bow our heads in prayer, sometimes I peek around under my eyelashes, watching to see who else has their eyes open. But I was praying tonight. Praying for Mom not to be home yet. Dad would be mad, but he would be O.K. alone.

"What's wrong?" Dad cried when he opened the door. His hair always sticks out, and his shirt rides up his back when he's been watching TV on the couch, so he looks just like a little kid. I could hear Mom's quick steps, and her shocked face appeared below his. She had on her nightgown.

"Carly, are you all right?"

I didn't have to answer. Officer Mary Jo Snelling answered everything and more. My parents just stared at me, and I stared at my feet. Officer Snelling seemed to be the only one of us who knew how to talk. After she told them what we'd done, she gave a lecture.

"As you know, Mr. and Mrs. Lewis, the juvenile-justice system is not punitive."

"Punitive?" Mom said.

"The ultimate goal of juvenile justice is rehabilitation."

"Rehabilitation?" My dad's eyebrows went up. He rubbed his hand over his face and groaned. "I knew I shouldn't have left her there, Bev. I had a bad feeling about the whole thing."

"We will file a report at the station, which you will have access to but which will not be released to the public. As we see it, this was just a case of a few kids horsing around, and no charges will be filed since they are minors, but I'm sure you'll want to have a talk with your daughter about this."

"I'm sure we will," said Mom, finally regaining her voice and fixing me with a cold stare.

Have a talk. That's an understatement. I wonder if it's possible to be lectured to death. You know, where the words bombard you to the point that your brain scrambles and your eyes roll back in your head and you just sink to the floor and breathe your last.

"Carly, a person is judged by the company she keeps."

"Carly, if those kids had decided to take drugs or rob a convenience store, would you have done that, too?"

"Carly, what if one of you kids had hit your head on the diving board, or if you'd injured yourself climbing that fence?"

"Carly, imagine what the rest of the faculty is thinking about the Lewis family."

Every time Dad looks at me, he seems to think of one more way to say how upset he is. And Mom just presses her lips tighter and tighter together.

So here I am. In my room. Until practically the end of time. I fully intend to do something crazy. I just don't know what it is yet.

Mom comes in, and Keesey dives under the bed just in time. Without speaking to me, Mom tosses a stack of laundry and a pile of papers at the foot of my bed. Then she leaves. I shuffle through the papers. An e-mail from Mr. Allen and the famous chapter by just Arlene. Dad printed them out for me. I pick up the e-mail from Mr. Allen.

Dear Young Scientists:

Another fascinating disaster has been submitted by Marty Bellows! Nice work, Marty.

## HUMONGOUS VOLCANIC ERUPTION

On May 18, 1980, Mount St. Helens in Washington State erupted with the force of 500 atomic bombs. Everything was destroyed for 230 square miles. Twenty-six lakes were filled with lava, about a million birds and animals were killed, and six million trees were knocked down. An ash cloud went 60,000 feet high, turned the skies dark for three days afterward, and circled the earth seven times before drifting to the ground.

My mother has written, "This looks interesting, Carly!" on the upper right-hand corner of the paper. Mom has also left me a brochure called "Getting Ready for the SAT." I sigh, tear it into thirty-two tiny pieces, and throw it away.

Finally, I leaf through Arlene's chapter. The first thing I notice is that there's no dialogue, which makes sense, I guess, since I usually write that part. Arlene must have meant for me to add it. Maybe Dad will let me borrow his laptop so I can write in dialogue. Then tonight I'll e-mail the chapter back to Arlene. Maybe later I can write a chapter by myself. Heaven knows I have the time, since I'm grounded basically forever.

As I settle on my bed, lazily scratching Keesey behind her ears, I realize that even though I've betrayed my best friend and I can't go anywhere for a month and my parents may never speak to me again, there is one ray of hope: Zack gave me back my glasses.

# chapter 12

$\mathbb{C}$ $\mathbb{C}$ $\mathbb{C}$ $\mathbb{C}$ $\mathbb{C}$ $\mathbb{C}$ $\mathbb{C}$ $\mathbb{C}$

## *Imprisoned in the Tower*

THE TOWER HAD A single window so high on the stone wall that Eva had to stand on a stool to see out of it. Perched on her tiptoes, she could see over the city's flat rooftops spreading from the crest of the hill straight across the plains to the pyramid, which was the only structure in Atlantis taller than the tower where she was now imprisoned.

There was nothing in this dark, tiny room but a narrow hammock. Eva was used to a goose-feather pillow and a quilt supplied by the royal silkworms. There was no writing desk, no closet full of tunics in every color of the rainbow, no mirror. Just damp stone walls and a cold stone floor.

She still couldn't figure out exactly what had happened. She had been curled up in the cave, asleep, and had opened her eyes sometime just after dawn to find herself face to face with one of her father's soldiers, a bare-chested thug in a brass headdress.

"I found one of them!" he shouted to his comrades. "Are you all right?" he asked solicitously as he helped her to her feet. "Your father and mother are very worried about you and your sister."

"I just bet they are." Eva yanked her arm free of his grasp and scrambled deeper into the cave, all the while glancing around, wondering where Lydia was hiding.

"Hey, come back here!" The soldier lunged after her, shouting over his shoulder, "I need backup in here!"

Three more soldiers rushed in. It was hopeless to try

to fight, but Eva kicked and punched with all her might, anyway. They carried her out of the cave, but at least she had the satisfaction of knowing that two of the soldiers were sore in some very key places.

They caught Sphinx, who had been grazing nearby. The one who'd found Eva wasn't polite any longer but held her by the arm so tightly it began to throb. He thrust his ugly jaw close to her and demanded, "Tell us where the mirror is."

"What mirror?" Eva drew a blank, then remembered the strange, small mirror Lydia had shown her.

"Don't act stupid. The Mirror of the Oracle. It disappeared the same day you and your sister did. Where's your sister?"

He didn't believe her when she swore she didn't know.

"We'll take you back to the king," he growled. "You can tell *him*. See how he likes that."

"See how my father likes it when I tell him you've treated me like a common criminal!" she snapped back. "He'll toss you in a dungeon to rot."

"Get on your horse," he said. "And no funny stuff."

But as soon as she mounted Sphinx, she jammed her heels into the mare's side and shouted, "Go!" Sphinx leaped forward down the steep, narrow path from the cave, stumbling and nearly throwing Eva. By the time the horse regained her footing, there were mounted soldiers on either side. They tied Eva's hands, and the soldier on the horse ahead took Sphinx's reins and led her down into the valley at a walk. Sphinx pinned her ears back, and when she tossed her head, Eva could see the whites of her eyes.

Where was Lydia? As the procession crossed the valley, Eva scanned the underbrush and tall grass. She studied the upper branches of the banyan tree when they passed it, thinking Lydia might be crouched on a limb behind a dappled screen of leaves.

Surely Lydia was following them, unseen, devising a plan to free her. Eva tried not to think about the fact that she herself was the one who always devised the plans. Lydia had been loyal and reliable once Eva told her what to do, but face it, she just wasn't an idea person.

Then she remembered the hours she and Lydia had spent trying to read each other's minds. True, they were never much good at it, but it was the only thing Eva could think of to do right now.

So as Sphinx approached the river, Eva closed her eyes and thought of Lydia. She chanted to herself, "Always together, never apart. Your thoughts are my thoughts . . . your heart is my heart." She made her mind go blank, clear to receive any message Lydia might send. For several seconds her mind's eye was a cool, blank field. And then she got something.

What she got was a color: blue.

And she knew that Lydia was not following along behind her or planning any daring rescue attempt. She was lost in the blue of the flying man's eyes. Eva sighed so loudly, one of the soldiers asked if she was all right.

Eva wondered about the mirror and why her father wanted it so badly. She wished she did have it—she'd have something to bargain with.

As soon as Sphinx forded the river and the procession passed through the royal vineyards, Eva shut her eyes again and summoned all the mental power she could muster into a one-word message to her sister: "HELP!" She imagined a big and brilliant splash pulsing across the sky, flying toward her sister swifter than a beam of light from the sun. She only hoped Lydia didn't think her message was "yelp" or "whelp" and imagine a confusing welter of unhappy puppies and have no idea what to do.

SO HERE SHE WAS, stuck in the tower. Her father had just declared war on another king and was meeting with the priest and chief warriors. Unless Eva could produce the Mirror of the Oracle, he was too busy to see her. Her mother had sent a message that she would be up for a visit soon and Eva "better think long and hard about what you have done, young lady."

No one had brought her anything to eat or drink except for a jug of water with a bug floating in it. She thought about her parents' dining table made of the four-hundred-year-old eucalyptus tree, the ram's horns her parents used to speak to one another, the dishes of steaming bread and duck meat, the succulent grapes and apples, and the soft, flavorful cheeses. She tried to ignore the unfamiliar gnawing in her stomach.

She stood on tiptoe and looked out the window, standing first on one foot and then the other when her calves began to cramp. Something was happening on top of the pyramid. Two people appeared to be building something, and they kept working, even after the purple clouds rolled in above the pyramid and the thunder and rains began. On her tiptoes, she watched, trying to figure out what it was.

# chapter 13

# *You're a Good Man, Charlie Brown*

EVERYONE KNOWS THE STORY of *You're a Good Man, Charlie Brown,* right? Charlie Brown is a failure. He can't kick the football. He can't fly a kite. His baseball team has never won a game. He is in love with the little red-haired girl, but she has never noticed him. Charlie Brown and all his friends are full of anxiety about their lives, Miss Norden says, even though they're only kids. Charlie Brown is everyman, says Miss Norden, which is why he is such an appealing character.

The first day of play practice, I wonder about this. I mean, I'm only twelve, but my life is full of anxiety, too. Most of the time I feel like a loser. I am so incredibly ordinary, just like Charlie Brown. Also, Zack Wingo has barely noticed me. I could be Charlie Brown.

I'd like to discuss this with Arlene, but we are sitting on opposite ends of the bleachers, and she's ignoring me. Zack is sitting in the first row with Marty, who got the part of understudy for Snoopy. Zack's drawing one of his trademark superhero megadoodles on the back page of his script. He's quiet and intense, very inside himself. I like his wavy, black hair, the freckle on his upper lip, the long, curly eyelashes girls would die for. I like that he doesn't seem to care what anyone thinks about him. I wish I didn't care so much.

Miss Norden has told us to go through our scripts and highlight our lines. It's the fourth week of October, and it's still about two hundred degrees in here, and most people are using their scripts to fan themselves. I forgot a highlighter, and

96

I'm thinking about asking Arlene if I can share hers and telling her I liked her chapter in our novel even though it had all adventure and no love. I never heard back from her after I added the dialogue to her chapter. I wonder if she ever got it and why she's ignoring me. She walks by me in the hall and acts as if she doesn't see me. She never sends me notes anymore. Last Friday she never even called about writing together. I wonder if she's still mad about the swimming pool thing.

I put my glasses on to climb down the rows of bleachers, past Zack and Marty. As I pass by, I hear Marty talking a mile a minute. He is so hyper, and his glasses are so thick he reminds me of a cartoon ant. Somebody told me Marty's dad took away his Nintendo for a month after our swimming fiasco. Zack keeps working on his superhero megadoodle and doesn't seem to be listening. I love that shiny silver layer of graphite that builds up on his pinky finger and the heel of his palm. I wonder whether it would rub off on me if I held his hand.

My heart is pounding, partly because of passing Zack and partly from nervousness over talking to Arlene. I sit beside her and put my glasses on my head. She pretends not to notice me. She puts her hair behind her ear, which still sticks out as much as ever, and then leaves her hand shading her face so I can't see it.

"Hi, Arlene."

The highlighter squeaks as she drags it across a line, and its sharp smell tickles my nostrils. I love the smell of highlighters. "Twenty-one," she whispers, counting her lines and ignoring me.

"That was a good chapter you wrote," I say. "Did you get the one I sent back?"

Arlene turns narrowed eyes on me. She circles her hand behind her ear again even though her hair is already there. "If you really thought it was good, you wouldn't have changed it all around."

"Huh? I thought you wanted me to put dialogue in."

"I cannot believe you rewrote my chapter. That was incredibly *presumptuous.*"

"Sorry. I didn't know—"

"Forget it." She looks down at her script again.

"We can put it back the way it was."

"That's O.K. Forget it."

"Arlene! I said I was sorry."

Arlene lets her shoulders relax and throws her hands in the air, sighing deeply. "O.K., fine, I admit it. The chapter was better after you changed it. Dad said so."

"He did?"

"Yeah, Dad says all artists should be open to change. It did need dialogue. Let's just forget about it." She stares at my glasses perched on my head and pushes hers up the bridge of her nose. "*Actually*, you know, glasses are only functional if they're in front of your eyes."

"Ha-ha." I pull them down and settle them cozily on my ears. It feels so great to be talking again. "So, was it hard, I mean, writing by yourself?"

Arlene rests her chin on her hand like she's an actor getting ready to give a speech. "At first the blank page was absolutely terrifying. But then I pretended to be you, sitting by the computer and wiggling my foot the way you do, and twirling a little piece of my hair the way you do, and saying, 'Let's have them fall in love.' And then I jumped on the bed and pretended to be me, and did some leg exercises, and stared at the ceiling, and said, 'Fall in love? How boring! We need some adventure!' And suddenly I was off and running."

She lends me her highlighter. All the bright yellow bars leap out at me, jazzy and heartstopping. Arlene reads Lucy's lines aloud with a whiny, bossy voice like in the Peanuts movies. She practices "You blockhead!" a dozen times, trying for the perfect inflection and accent. Accents make me think of Whitney, and I have kind of a pang in my stomach. I saw Whitney in the hall today.

"Hey, Carl," she said in her best North Carolina accent. "How ya doin'?"

"O.K."

"Cute top. You're looking good, girl."

"Thanks. You, too," I said.

"You want to do something Saturday, go see a movie or something?" she added. "I quit smoking, you know. I turned over a new leaf. Maybe your mom could drive us."

"I'm still grounded," I said. I didn't tell her that Mom and Dad had basically told me I couldn't see Whitney anymore. I got my midterm grades and have straight C's. Miss Norden wrote a note in the comments section that says, "Carly can do better." Mom and Dad were so furious, I have been trying to stay out of their way. But I wondered if I could figure out how to sneak out and go to a movie with Whitney, anyway.

Later at my locker I overheard Tracy say to Ashley that Whitney was getting on her nerves, and Ashley agreed that she was tired of her, too. They both thought she tried to steal all the attention for herself. I felt sorry for Whitney. I also wondered if that was why she was being nice to me.

Now I watch Arlene's lips as she silently recites some of her lines. She'll probably have all of them memorized by tomorrow. I think she has a photographic memory. I notice that her hair is stringy and she's still dressed like a kid from elementary school in one of those Peter Pan blouses and a plaid jumper that's too short for her long, skinny legs. I never used to notice what she wore. I never cared.

"What do you think about everyone in the play having anxiety about their lives, even though they're little kids?" I ask her. "I feel that we're under too much pressure. Don't you?"

"Dad says happiness doesn't make for interesting drama. That's why Lucy is the best part. She's *flawed.*" She lifts the highlighter from my fingers, underlines her next line, and hands it back. Arlene doesn't find things confusing the way I do. Something either makes for good drama, or it doesn't. It's so simple. I like that. I want things to be like that again.

Once Mom dragged me to Belk's to buy a wedding gift for someone, and she held a crystal glass up to the light and said to the saleslady, "This one is *flawed*." I tried squinting at the glass to see what she meant, and I finally made out a tiny, wandering line, like a river that isn't sure where to go. Mom said there are flaws in diamonds, too, which can't be seen with the naked eye. So Lucy being flawed means she's not perfect. Isn't Charlie Brown flawed, too, as well as Schroeder, and Linus, and Sally, and Snoopy? Aren't we all flawed?

"Attention, people!" Miss Norden places a stack of handouts on the podium at the foot of the bleachers and claps for our attention. Her hair is damp and curly at the temples, and her sleeveless denim blouse has dark half-moons under the arms. "*Charlie Brown* will be produced as part of our Winter Festival fund-raiser, so we have only six weeks to rehearse. You'll need to know the songs in two weeks, and all your lines by the middle of November. Unfortunately, we have no budget for costumes, so everyone is responsible for his or her own. I'm still looking for volunteers to be our makeup, prop, and set people. I hope everyone is looking forward to this. Doing a play can be one of the most memorable experiences of your life. Any questions before I pass out the rehearsal schedule?"

A girl with green hair and black fingernail polish raises her hand. "Can I go to the bathroom?"

Miss Norden sighs. "Go ahead." She calls on someone else. "Yes?"

"How much longer will this take? I have volleyball practice in fifteen minutes."

Miss Norden sighs more deeply. "If play practice conflicts with volleyball practice, you will need to choose whether to be in the play or whether to play volleyball."

Marty raises his hand. "Is this for a grade, I mean, do we get extra credit in language arts for this?"

"Grades are not the most important things in life, Mr. Bellows!" Miss Norden throws her hands up in exasperation so abruptly she knocks the stack of rehearsal schedules off the podium. There is complete silence. Rehearsal schedules are scattered over the gym floor. A few stragglers float softly down like leaves.

"O.K., thanks," says Marty in a small voice. We all know he will think twice before bringing up grades again.

Miss Norden drops to her hands and knees to gather the handouts. After a minute, Arlene puts her script aside and gets down to help. I wait only a few seconds before I start helping, too, even though I swore to hate Miss Norden forever. I guess I don't really hate her. I keep feeling there is something she wants from us, more than good grades, that I would like to give to her if only I knew what it was.

"Thank you, ladies," Miss Norden says gruffly as we hand her our wrinkled stacks. She runs her hand through her hair, takes a deep breath, and then acts like nothing happened. Today, she says, we will use our scripts to do a "read-through" of the first act. "I'll need Charlie Brown, Snoopy, Lucy, Schroeder, Linus, and Sally onstage with their scripts," she says. "And let's have the chorus stand at backstage right."

I sneak a look at Zack. He folds his script in half, stuffs it in his back jeans pocket, and crosses to the stage with Marty half running, still talking, by his side.

"Earth to Carly." Arlene has said something to me. I have no idea what it was.

"What?" We walk together across the gym floor and climb the steps to the stage.

"I said are you still grounded?"

"Yeah. For two and a half more weeks."

"How excruciatingly traumatic." Arlene throws her hand over her brow in a dramatic gesture. "I suppose the only solution is to keep e-mailing chapters."

"Yeah, O.K."

"It's your turn. I wrote about Eva in the tower, so now my suggestion is for you to write about Lydia."

I swallow. "I've never written a chapter by myself." We help Miss Norden arrange folding chairs in a semicircle on the stage. Metallic clanging sounds echo in the high-ceilinged gym.

"Send her on a quest." Arlene unfolds a chair upside down, and I turn it right side up for her. "E-mail a chapter to me on Saturday sometime."

"O.K.," I say. "Maybe I'll have her fall in love." I try to focus on Arlene's round glasses. I avoid looking at Zack, who is standing right beside me.

"Let me have Lucy and Schroeder right here," says Miss Norden. Two chairs squeal against the floor as she yanks them together.

Arlene sits in one of the chairs.

"And Linus and Sally right here." Two more chairs squeal against the floor.

"So," says Zack, "did you get in trouble after the deal at the pool?"

"Yeah," I say. *Say something else,* my brain screams at me. He must be reeling with my clever repartee. Oh, man, I wish one of those trapdoors would open right here on the stage and swallow me up. I desperately want to say something to him, but my brain is one vast, blank wall of panic. "Did you?" I finally choke out.

"Grounded for two weeks, no TV or computer, and write a letter of apology to the police department."

"I'm grounded for a month."

"A month? That sounds extreme."

"Carly Lewis! Please get into position with the rest of the chorus." Miss Norden's voice ends our conversation. My cheeks start to ignite. It takes about a year to walk backstage, with hoots and laughter ricocheting off every surface.

"Let's take it from the top," says Miss Norden. "How many of you know what that means, 'take it from the top'?"

I raise my hand and see that Zack has his up, too. I get goose bumps. A girl with red hair, who plays Sally, has raised her hand. Arlene of course has also raised hers, giving me a look that says, "We are the elite who know what 'take it from the top' means." Everybody else just sits there. Miss Norden explains that it means "start at the beginning." The cast starts to read the lines from the opening scene.

I soar through play practice in a warm haze of joy.

*He started a conversation with me.* Maybe he actually likes me.

JOSH, THE KID WHOSE mom has cancer in her eye, is sleeping over with Matt on Friday night. Josh puts his elbows on the table and doesn't use a napkin. He skips all the green vegetables and serves himself so much rice there is hardly any left for the rest of us, but Mom and Dad don't say anything.

"My mom only has one eye," says Josh. "She's wearing a patch just like a pirate."

"We know," says my mom.

Dad says, "Soon she'll have a prosthetic eye that will look so much like her real eye, I bet you'll forget which one is real and which one isn't."

"I won't forget," says Josh. "If she cries, I bet real tears won't come out."

"Yes, they will," says my dad. "You wait and see. Your mom is very brave, you know. You should be proud of her."

"I guess so," says Josh.

Josh doesn't want to go down to the basement after dinner is over. He wants to stay in the family room and tell stuff to my parents, just like Arlene. Josh has a habit of doing handstands the whole time he's talking to you. Mom reminds him that he just ate, but he says it's O.K., he's got an iron stomach and has never thrown up in his whole life.

I'm still grounded, but Matt is allowed to invite Josh. Mom and Dad can listen to Josh and be so understanding and act like he's special, but they can't do the same thing with their own daughter. Besides, my parents believe the stuff he is saying, while I'm smart enough to know that it's all a bunch of lies. Have you ever met a kid who has never thrown up in his whole life?

"I'm probably going to be on *You Guessed It.*" Josh does another handstand, planting his hands and flinging his legs in the air. He only stays like that for about one second before his legs fall back down.

"Really? When?" Mom is scraping dishes.

"I'm not sure exactly when, but see, I invented this hat that squirts water to cool you down when you're hot. You hook it up to the hose." He plants his hands, flings his feet, and they fall down again. "That's what they do on *You Guessed It,* you know. They try to guess what you invented. And I'm definitely going to be on."

"So you walk around attached to a hose?" I say, rolling my eyes at Mom as I help her load the dishwasher. Mom gives me a look that says, "Be nice."

Josh throws his legs up into the air so hard he lands on his back with a thud. This must happen fairly often because he doesn't even say, "Ow." He just stands up and holds his arms over his head again, getting ready for the next handstand.

"You're a very enterprising young man," says my dad as he turns on the news. "Be sure and let us know when you're on so we can watch."

"Yeah," I say. "You do that, Josh." I pinch my lips together to keep from guffawing loudly.

"I definitely will." Josh, upside down, sticks his tongue out at me.

Mom and Dad sit down to watch the news, where a meteorologist is tracking a large, late-season hurricane out in the Atlantic that might be headed for the North Carolina coast. Josh and Matt both call me a dingleberry and run down to the basement to play Nintendo. I go to my room and slam my door. They are so immature. How do boys get from being Matt and Josh to being Zack? I stare out the window at the reddish orange oak leaves, which are starting to turn brown. There is a whisper of coolness in the evening now, and it's getting dark earlier.

Dad is letting me use his laptop tonight to write the chapter that I'm going to e-mail to Arlene. I get myself settled on the bed, sitting cross-legged, and get the laptop all set up to the word processing program. I set the margins and line spacing, then test several different fonts and choose a fancy one.

The sky has turned a lovely color of navy blue, and I can see one star, which Dad has said is not a star but Venus. I touch my eyelid, thinking about Josh's mom. I think about the freckle on Zack Wingo's upper lip. I think about getting a snack. I look at the clock. It's seven-thirty. Zack was right. A month of this is going to be intolerable.

I've heard that lots of writers work with their cats in their laps. I look under the bed for Keesey, because I let her in this afternoon. I know she's in my room somewhere. I finally find her curled up in an old baby-doll cradle in my closet. I drag her out and onto the bed with her hind feet hanging down. She doesn't want to sit on my lap. I use brute force to hold her with one hand while I type with one finger of the other. She is growling, very low and quiet, her ears laid back and her tail thumping the bed in an angry rhythm. She sheds more when she's mad, and I have cat hair on my shirt, in between my fingers, and lying like mosquito netting on the keyboard of Dad's laptop. She starts wiggling around and digging into the bedspread with her hind legs, growling more loudly. I tighten my grip on her front leg. I don't let go until she tries to bite me, and then she tears off, right across the keyboard, typing ";kutensq23!" as she runs. I blow on the keys, which sends a cascade of cat hair up into my face.

Cleopatra and Emma and even Pollyanna and Wendy glare at me without a shred of sympathy.

*Stay in Neverland if you want to, but the rest of us are leaving,* Wendy says.

*No matter what happens, one must keep a stiff upper lip and carry on,* says Emma.

*You give up too easily,* says Cleopatra. *Once I snuck into Marc Antony's room rolled up inside a rug.*

*Look on the bright side,* says Pollyanna. *There must be a bright side somewhere.*

"Quiet!" I growl. I actually wish Matt and Josh would burst into my room spraying gunfire sound effects or making loud flatulent noises using their hands cupped in their armpits. Suddenly I realize I'm afraid to start. I'm afraid I won't have any ideas of my own, that all this time everything has been Arlene's vision, and I have truly been her measly sidekick. She wrote a whole chapter without me. I stare at the blank screen and think about where we last saw Lydia. She was with the flying man and had just gone to the cave to discover that Eva was gone. Now what?

# chapter 14

## Lost in the Blue Eyes of the Flying Man

LYDIA AND LEORBUR WENT down to the river's edge to gather reeds. They planned to weave a basket that could carry a person beneath the balloon. Leorbur had carved the burl of a tree to form the floor. To it he'd attached strong, whiplike, bamboo shoots at short intervals. Now he was showing Lydia how to weave reeds in and out between them.

Leorbur had slim, agile fingers. He didn't talk much, except to suggest, practically every hour, that as soon as the basket was complete, they should look for her sister again. Lydia agreed, although she didn't know why he cared so much. She was perfectly happy, for the time being, with him. She was hungry and knew her tunic was torn and dirty, and she had leaves and sticks in her hair. But the memories of her previous life as a princess had grown dim in the space of one day. That existence now seemed aimless and childish, embarrassing in its luxury and ease. This was a life with purpose. The morning glided past like a silver heron in the sky.

The basket, when finished, would be large enough for two people. Leorbur also had an idea to install two wooden seats. He and Lydia worked through the day, taking breaks to rest or eat chunks of bread Leorbur tore from a loaf in his knapsack.

"When did you first start trying to fly?" she asked him as she gnawed at the hunk of brown bread he had given her.

"I cannot remember a time in my life when I wasn't trying to fly. I was the youngest prince in the palace."

"You're a prince?"

"Yes, my father is King Eumaeus, ruler of Southern Atlantis."

"Oh." Lydia swallowed. She was glad she hadn't told Leorbur who she was, because her father had been at war with his father for over a year.

"When I was five or six, I used to dream of flying every night. My older brothers and sisters made fun of me. They told me I would never succeed at flying." Leorbur straightened and watched the purple velvet rain clouds unroll across the afternoon sky. "In my dream there was a terrible storm. But I could float above the clouds. Sometimes I had wings; other times I was riding in a basket like this." He picked up another reed. "I *am* going to succeed. I will keep trying until I do."

"Why did you leave your father's kingdom?"

"As the youngest son, I was not in line to inherit any land. When I was twelve, I was assigned to fight on my father's war chariot. I suppose I am a coward, because I left home."

Lydia did not think Leorbur was a coward. She had a great desire for Leorbur to notice her—to ask a question that showed he had an interest in who she was and what she thought. At the same time, what she admired most about him was his devotion to flying.

A dark sheet of rain approached from behind the ridge, and a faint, drumming sound began to swell. Leorbur stopped and listened. "Not just rain," he said. "Hoofbeats."

Lydia could hear the hoofbeats now, too. She gasped. "Soldiers! They may be searching for me. I need to hide!" She looked wildly around.

"Why?" he said, puzzled.

She crouched and pulled the basket over herself. "Pretend

you're working on the bottom," she hissed from between the woven reeds.

Leorbur was planing the bottom of the basket when Lydia heard the cacophony of many horses galloping, slowing, stopping, snorting. The basket was tightly woven, but she glimpsed the flash of a fetlock in a tiny splinter of light between two reeds.

"Ho there. King Avalach is searching for his daughter" came an arrogant but nasal male voice. "He has placed a reward of one hundred pounds of raw orichalcum on her head. Have you seen her?"

"I couldn't say," said Leorbur. "What does she look like?"

Lydia held her breath, annoyed. Why not just say he hadn't seen a single person since sunup? What was wrong with him? She saw the pink gleam of a polished copper spur flash in the sliver of light near her eye. Sweat trickled down her temple. It was hot and close inside this basket. And suddenly something very strange pulsed like a bolt of lightning to her brain. Strange words. KELP IN THE SHOWER.

"Princess Lydia is thirteen years old, with almond eyes and tawny skin and beautifully braided auburn hair. She would be wearing only the finest jeweled sandals and a tunic of the most exquisite silken cloth. The king also has reason to believe that she has in her possession an extremely valuable mirror—the Mirror of the Oracle."

The mirror! Lydia sucked in her breath, but again the strange message forced its way over the wall of her fear, crowding out her thoughts. KELP IN THE SHOWER.

"I have seen only one girl in the recent past," said Leorbur thoughtfully. A drop of burning sweat slid into Lydia's right eye. "The girl I have seen does not fit that description. This girl has sticks and leaves in her hair, a torn tunic, and scratches all over her face. She certainly did not have a mirror that I could see—I do not believe she was even wearing shoes."

KELP IN THE SHOWER. Leorbur was giving her up, and still that message muscled its way past all other thoughts. It must be Eva.

"Oh," said the soldier with bored disappointment. "A peasant girl, perhaps driven from her home by the floods. That would not have been Princess Lydia."

"I suppose not," said Leorbur cheerfully. "But I certainly will keep an eye out, as I could use a hundred pounds of raw orichalcum."

"Thank you, sir," said the soldier. "Should you see her, you need simply deliver her to the nearest guardhouse to receive your reward."

"I will keep that in mind. Good day."

"Good day to you."

Through the sliver of space, Lydia saw the soldiers drive their mounts forward, and then heard splashing and rocks against the horses' hoofs as they crossed the river shallows. She folded her fingers around the mirror, still in her pocket, and didn't move even after the sounds had whispered away to nothing.

KELP IN THE SHOWER. Crouched in the heat inside the overturned basket, Lydia closed her eyes and tried to open her mind to Eva's message. It made no sense. Of course, when they'd practiced mind reading, it had never made any sense. Her messages to Eva had always come out as a color, while Eva's to her had always come out as some jumbled rhyming phrases.

Jumbled rhyming phrases. She squeezed her eyes shut. KELP IN THE SHOWER. WHELP IN THE BOWER. YELP IN THE TOWER. HELP IN THE TOWER.

HELP, I'M IN THE TOWER!

Her eyes flew open. Thunder cracked.

The basket tipped up briefly, but instead of Leorbur

letting her out, he crawled inside with her just as rain splatted all around. The Atlanteans had been making boats of reeds for hundreds of years, so the basket was quite watertight. Lydia and Leorbur sat facing each other, relatively dry and breathing in each other's damp warmth as torrents of water gushed from the black clouds above.

"Should there be a flash flood, we could turn the basket upright and be quite seaworthy," observed Leorbur. His legs were folded against Lydia's, and she could feel the fuzz of hair on his calves. "I didn't give you away, did you notice? Yet I didn't lie. Princess Lydia."

Something in his demeanor had changed. What was it? Then it dawned on her—he had at last noticed her. He was paying attention. The thought made her dizzy.

He touched her wild, unbraided hair. "All along, I thought you were the other one, your sister, Eva. Because of your hair."

"No, I'm Lydia." Her voice was a squeak. "That's why you were so anxious to find my sister?"

"Yes. *You* were the one I liked. And all along you were right here with me."

Time seemed to stop. No one had ever liked her better than Eva. KELP IN THE SHOWER.

"But," she said, "I've just found out that Eva is a prisoner in the tower. We can't wait to finish the basket—we have to go save her now."

"There's no need. We're together, and we have to fly; that's all there's time for. Flying."

Lydia was about to answer when he put his index finger on her lips. For a moment he pretended his finger was a bird as it took flight, exploring her eyelashes, her nose, and her chin. Water crept under the basket, washed beneath her toes. Then his lips met hers, separated only by a single drop of warm, fresh rain.

# chapter 15

## Chalk Squares

ON SUNDAY NIGHT I can't sleep. Moonlight bathes my bedroom walls, and a stiff breeze rattles the leaves on the oak tree outside the window, creating shifting light patterns, like a flock of Tinker Bells. Something that a lot of people forget about Tinker Bell is that she had a very unpleasant disposition and even tried to kill Wendy.

I feel a small but distinct shaking of my bed. There is a faint, tinkling sound, like wind chimes. Over on the bookshelf my cat figurines are trembling. On the shelf right above, Pollyanna, in her frilly pantalets and corkscrew curls, pitches forward onto her sweet, painted face. I lie frozen, not daring to breathe. What was that?

THE NEXT DAY AFTER play practice, we're all sitting on the front steps of the school waiting for our parents to pick us up, and we talk about the big news. Last night, although the hurricane changed course and veered back out into the ocean, North Carolina had a teeny, tiny earthquake. This morning Dad read out loud from the newspaper about some lady's china teacup collection falling out of her breakfront and smashing. And a man's false teeth, soaking in a glass of water on his bathroom sink, crashed to the tile floor.

"Did you feel it?" says Marty Bellows. "My collection of Star Wars characters did this little tap dance."

"That was definitely weird," Zack agrees.

"Yeah," I say. The sun has dropped behind the big maple tree next to the bicycle rack, but the marble steps are still warm beneath my jean skirt. I'm sitting with Arlene, and Zack and Marty are sitting together a few feet away. I spend hours planning conversations with Zack but can never think of anything to say when he's actually around. I start to tell about the storybook Pollyanna doll falling over but decide against it because then Zack will know I have one. Before I say anything at all, Whitney comes out and plops herself down right between us. She smells like cigarette smoke and perfume. I guess she didn't quit smoking for very long.

She's volunteered to be in charge of sets. Today while Miss Norden was rehearsing a scene, I noticed Whitney over in the corner of the auditorium sketching something on a big sheet of plywood. Zack walked over to look at it. They talked awhile, and then Zack kneeled beside her and pointed. He slid the pencil from her fingers and changed something. Whitney nodded and smiled, and then Zack had to leave because Miss Norden called, "I need Schroeder and Snoopy onstage now!"

Zack headed across the gym. So did Marty Bellows. The guy who was supposed to play Snoopy got put on academic probation, and now Marty is playing the part.

I walked over to see what Whitney was working on. It was a side view of Snoopy's doghouse.

"Hey," I said. "That's good. I didn't know you were an artist."

"I try to keep it to myself," she said, sitting back on her heels to compare the shape of the door to a picture she was copying.

"How come?" I said.

"It's not cool, I guess." She looked up at me. "How come you quit wearing the makeup? It looked good."

I would rather eat a bug than tell her Mom still wouldn't let me, so I just shrugged. She looked hurt and turned back to her sketch.

I wanted to talk to her more, but suddenly a boy's voice flowed like a cool wave from the stage to the far corners of the auditorium. This boy's voice was so good that I got goose bumps. Everybody in the auditorium stopped what they were doing.

It was Marty Bellows, standing very straight, his glasses glinting like mirrors every time he leaned close to the mike. Everyone just stared. I know this sounds weird, but while he's singing, it's like everything in the world stops. Every cell in your body wakes up to that big voice coming out of that little guy. When he finished, there was complete silence for about ten seconds, like no one wanted ordinary life to start up again. And then the whole cast and crew started clapping.

"Wow," said Whitney. "He's awesome. Who would've guessed?"

Miss Norden, standing at the foot of the stage steps, took off her glasses and scrubbed her eyes with a tissue. "Very nice, Martin," she said and then blew her nose.

In a movie the cheerleaders would all suddenly be wild about Marty, and he would be rocketed out of nerdhood forever. But in real life, play practice is over, and we're sitting on the steps waiting for our parents, and he's still plain old Marty, Zack Wingo's hyperactive sidekick. The cheerleaders still ignore him. He drums his fingers on the steps and checks his watch about every thirty seconds. He's still two steps behind in every conversation. Arlene is the only one who quizzes him about his singing. It turns out he learned in the choir at church.

There are about five different groups of kids who stay after school, all waiting on the steps. On sitcoms they show rich and poor kids being friends, black and white kids who hang out at each other's houses, and jocks and artsy kids sitting together at lunch, and I wish it were true, but at our school it's just not like that. We stay in our groups, as if there were chalk lines drawn down the steps and we're not allowed to cross over them.

Sitting on the top step are the guys who play football, and beside them are the cheerleaders. Tracy is a cheerleader. She acts as if she's never seen me before in her entire life, even though her wet hair dripped down my arm in the back of the squad car the night of the swimming fiasco.

The girls' soccer team has its own imaginary chalk square, and the kids who work on the school newspaper have theirs. Then there's us, the kids in the play. I think about the imaginary chalk lines dividing the groups on the steps, and I'm not sure I really belong in any of them. I mean, I'm sitting here with the people in the play, but some of them are even more bizarre than Arlene.

If I had a group, what would it be? Girls who wish they were descended from mermaid royalty instead of living with their actual families? Girls who have dolls in their rooms that give them advice? That sounds like a group, maybe, of one. I want to fit in, but I love my daydreams so much. Am I that weird?

I am jolted back to the marble steps when I overhear Whitney ask Zack if he ever worried about the Big One back in California. He says, "Yeah, sure, of course." She says, "Me, too. How can you not?" They both laugh, and it looks as if they're in their own little chalk box, together, without anyone else.

What's the Big One? I wonder. And then Marty saves me because he pokes Zack in the arm. "Are you talking about the humongous earthquake that's going to make California fall into the ocean?" he says.

"Yeah," says Whitney.

"If you live in California, people talk about the Big One all the time," explains Zack. "It's just something everybody lives with. Mass destruction."

"Oh," says Marty. "Like the one that hit San Francisco in 1906."

"I guess," says Whitney.

"I found out about that," Marty continues, with a glance in my direction, "when I was doing research for the Young Scientists Club."

"The Young Scientists Club?" Whitney laughs and leans on Zack's shoulder.

"Yeah," says Marty. "Carly's in it. We're doing a time line of natural disasters. It's pretty cool. Are you going to the meeting tomorrow morning, Carly?"

"Yeah, sure." I nod.

Whitney is rolling her eyes in Zack's direction.

"*Actually,* to be completely accurate about the Big One, there are fault lines where geological plates rub up next to each other," Arlene tells Marty. "The San Andreas fault is an example. A number of geologists believe the geological plates west of the San Andreas fault could collapse into the Pacific during an earthquake that exceeds 7.8 on the Richter scale."

"That is partially correct," says Marty, "except most scientists prefer the moment magnitude scale to the Richter scale for earthquakes above seven."

"I personally believe the Big One will simply be a natural phenomenon," Arlene continues, "but you can't deny the dramatic possibilities offered by the theory that it will be God's way of punishing those who have hedonistic lifestyles."

"That's not what I would call a scientific approach," says Marty. He turns to Zack. "The Young Scientists Club is going on an all-night field trip to see a meteor shower."

"Really?" says Zack.

"How fascinating." Whitney sneaks a look at Zack, but he pretends not to notice that she's making fun of Marty and Arlene. "So, Arlene," she continues, "are you going to the seventh-grade dance next Friday night?"

Arlene glances at her, confused, and pushes her glasses up her nose. "Dance?" she says.

"Yeah," says Whitney. "You should go. Lots of guys will want to dance with you."

"No, Carly and I are writing a novel. We always work on it Friday night," says Arlene. "By the way, I almost forgot." She shoves a printout into my lap. "Here's the chapter you e-mailed me. I made a few changes."

"Oh," I say. It's hard to focus on it because I'm still thinking about the dance and the Big One and Zack's and Whitney's shoulders touching and Whitney making fun of Arlene. I look down at the page Arlene has given me and scan the first line. It's different. She's changed my first line.

"Oh," I say again. Why would she do that? Heat crawls up my neck, spreading to my earlobes. It feels like both my ears are on fire.

"Carly!" My mother has pulled up and leans out the van window, waving. I jump up and run down the steps, shoving the chapter into my backpack. I don't say good-bye to Arlene.

But as I slam the door and buckle the seat belt, Mom calls out to her. "Hi, Arlene. How are you, sweetie?"

"Jolly well," calls Arlene in a fake English accent, which causes my mother to break into peals of laughter. I, on the other hand, would like to disappear into an earthquake-sized hole.

"Good. I bet you're just great in the play. We can't wait to come watch you." Mom beams at her.

"Oh, thank you, I'm sure," says Arlene, with yet a new accent, gesturing grandly like a diva from Queens. As we pull away, I see Whitney fall sideways against Zack, laughing uncontrollably.

"Arlene is a riot," says Mom. "Now, that's a girl who knows who she is." Mom pats my leg. Fortunately, we're out of the school parking lot, so no one sees this. "So, how was play practice?"

"O.K.," I say. I give in to temptation and pull Arlene's rewrite of my chapter out of my backpack and scan the first page. It appears she has not only changed the first sentence, she's changed the second one, too. And the third. I rifle to the end of the chapter. She's completely erased the paragraph where Lydia and Leorbur kiss.

I look out the window. There is a loud, angry roaring like Niagara Falls in my head. When I get home, I plan to tear Arlene's chapter into little, teeny pieces and stuff it in an envelope and mail it to her with a note in all capital letters that says, "I'M NEVER SPEAKING TO YOU AGAIN."

"Carly!" Mom sounds annoyed.

"Huh?" I look over.

"Did you hear what I said?"

"No. Sorry."

"I said," Mom says patiently, "I won that grant I was trying to get, and the weekend right after the play, I have to make a speech about my research in Raleigh. Dad has a seminar that same weekend, so I've arranged for you to stay with Arlene."

"Arlene?" How could Mom do that, just make arrangements without even asking me, as if I'm a little kid? I feel like I've got boiling water behind my eyes.

"Carly," Mom says. "What in the world is wrong with you?"

"NOTHING!" It comes out as almost a shout. "Sorry," I add quickly. I hate Arlene and her superior attitude and the way she says, "*Actually*," all the time to correct people. I hate the way the kids make fun of us. I look out the window as we drive by the neighborhood pool. The parking lot is empty. The white-and-blue steps to the high dive seem to climb into nowhere since they've taken down the board. A chill runs through me as I remember the night we snuck into the pool.

Mom pulls in to the biology building parking lot, turns off the engine, and looks over at me. "What's going on with you and Arlene, anyway? Are you girls getting along these days?"

"Not exactly," I mumble, then immediately regret it. Now she'll ask a million questions. And with that many questions, she's bound to turn up something I did wrong.

Mom gets out of the van. "Do you want to talk about it?" Her face looks tired, but her eyes are warm and concerned.

"Not really." I glance down, not meaning to look at the manuscript, but there it is on my lap.

Mom's eyes flicker at it. "Walk in with me, Carly. Come on. I'm doing some time-lapse photography, and I just need to check the focus on the fluorescent microscope."

I stuff the manuscript in my backpack and follow Mom into the building. We pass Eldon the skeleton, who holds a trick-or-treat bag and wears a yellow dress and a Snow White mask. Dad says biologists have a sick sense of humor.

"I was twelve once, you know," Mom says as we walk down the long, pristine hall. "Believe it or not, I did have friends among the primitive life forms that walked the earth during that era. Maybe I can help you."

"I don't think so," I say. "You didn't write novels," I add, as if this explains why I don't think Mom can help.

Without answering, Mom unlocks the door to her lab and flips the light switch. Light spills over slabs of gray counter-tops, microscopes, petri dishes with tiny tadpoles, bouncy purple stools on wheels, and a refrigerator with *Far Side* car-toons taped on it. The clock, instead of having numbers, shows twelve tadpoles in different stages of development. On the white marker board Mom has three separate columns: "Things to Do," "Wish List," and "Solutions to Make."

"Well," says Mom at last. "What's this about, writing or friendship?"

I stare at some blind tadpoles in a petri dish as they blun-der around and bump into each other. "Well . . ." I hesitate. She's got me there. "Friendship, I guess."

"And what's the problem?"

"Arlene's just getting on my nerves." I blush as I realize that's exactly what I heard Tracy say about Whitney only last week. She sounded shallow, like someone who wasn't a good friend at all.

"Well, friendship is a very fragile thing," says Mom. She puts a petri dish under a microscope, takes off her glasses, and stares through the eyepiece, turning the knob to bring the tadpoles into focus.

"People make fun of Arlene," I finally say. "And of me, too, since I'm friends with her."

"H'm. What do you think about that?" As if the question weren't important, Mom continues looking through the micro-scope, but I can see the sinews of her knuckles on the focus knob, so I know it is important.

"It's mean," I say, with an offhand shrug. "They shouldn't do it."

"O.K. Well, is there anything you can do?" Mom suddenly

looks up, puts on her glasses, and fixes me with a penetrating gaze.

"Mom, *I'm* not doing it. Besides, I told you, they make fun of me, too, when I'm with her." I'm starting to feel uncomfortable with this conversation. "The thing is, Arlene's so bossy, and she thinks she knows everything, and she's always correcting people. And I think her accents are stupid."

Without answering, Mom heads over to the small darkroom where the fluorescent microscope is kept. A minute or so later she pokes her head out the door and waves me in. "Carly, come take a look at this," she says, just as if we're not in the middle of a conversation about something completely different. I go into the darkroom, and she shuts the door behind me. "I'm measuring the growth of neurons in the tadpole's brain. We dye the neurons a bright red to track their growth. Tonight this tadpole is blind. By tomorrow morning it will be able to see. If you look, you'll see the neurons starting to make their way from the eye toward the brain. It's miraculous."

As soon as my eyes have adjusted, I bend over the microscope and squint down at the tiny tadpole. Because it's in water mixed with anesthesia, it lies perfectly still. Its greenish gold body is translucent. I can even see its heart beating in an elongated sac of tissue. From its large, round eye, easily visible because it looks like a doughnut, I see a bright, wavy line with branches that look like tiny streams on a map, wandering in the direction of the tadpole's brain. The streams are bright red, the color of the dye Mom uses.

"I have the camera set up to take a picture every few hours, so by tomorrow morning I'll have time-lapsed photographs capturing the entire process."

"What does this have to do with anything?" I stand up and reach under my glasses to rub my eyes, try to focus.

"Well," says Mom patiently, "what we're doing, sweetie, is studying how different substances affect the growth of neurons. Tadpole brains are easier to study than human brains because they're so simple."

"No lie."

"What if we could make the neurons branch more? Think about what we can do, in time, for kids who have problems caused by faulty wiring in their brains." We go back out into the lab, shutting the darkroom door behind us. Mom turns out the lights. "Anyway. Back to you and Arlene. Maybe you are developing different interests and don't have as much in common as you used to. But you have been best friends since second grade. You can't just stand by and let other people be cruel. You need to stand up for her . . . and for yourself."

I stare at Mom. The lab is quiet and dark, and her words hang in the air. I think about the bright, neon strands of neurons, like tiny, red streams trying to feel their way from the eyes to the brains of the tadpoles. I feel like one of these tadpoles—almost, but not quite, able to see what life is all about. Any day, I think, all the connections will be made, and everything will leap into focus.

I follow Mom back to the van, finding it impossible to imagine myself saying anything about Arlene to Whitney. It seems even scarier than being in the play. So as we pull into the garage, I change the subject. "Can I go to the seventh-grade dance on Friday night?"

"I don't think so, Carly," Mom says as she shuts the van door.

"Why not?"

"You'll still be grounded next weekend."

"I've already been grounded for almost three weeks." I yank my backpack out of the van and slam the door. "I've learned my lesson. Everybody at school thinks that you guys grounding me for a month is extreme. Why can't I go to the dance?"

Mom climbs the steps from the garage to the kitchen. She looks at me thoughtfully and sighs. "I know it seems like a long time, but Dad and I wouldn't be good parents if we let you out of your punishment just to go to a dance. I guess the answer has to be no."

I glare at her and stalk up the stairs.

"All those midterm C's you brought home indicate you have plenty of studying you can do. And, Carly, I ordered some practice SAT tests. Maybe you could take one this weekend."

"Arggghhh!" I let out a scream of frustration and run down the hall to my room, slamming the door behind me. I am so mad at Mom that when I write the answers to my homework problems, the pencil practically cuts through the paper. Every time I talk to Mom about something, she makes me feel like a bad person. She and Dad were so perfect I could just HURL.

I get out Arlene's rewrite of my chapter, and instead of tearing it up, I fold the pages and shove them into the very bottom drawer of my desk. I guess I'm not going to rip it up, but I don't know what I'm going to say to Arlene yet. When I go on-line, I see I have another e-mail from Mr. Allen, reminding us about the Young Scientists Club meeting before school tomorrow morning.

IT IS KIND OF a surprise when I get to Mr. Allen's classroom. Craig and Marty and Amy are there, but so are lots of others. A few of the popular girls, including Tracy, have joined. They sit in the front row and cross their legs and toss their hair over their shoulders and smile at Mr. Allen. They haven't written up disasters and act as if they will be able to go on the field trip without doing it. Arlene also comes, although I didn't invite her. I don't sit next to her. She has printed out a five-page, single-spaced paper on the strongest earthquake ever recorded—8.4 on the Richter scale—which struck Prince William Sound in Alaska in 1964. And believe it or not, Zack and Whitney are both there, I guess because of the Big One.

"Welcome to the Young Scientists Club, everyone," says Mr.

Allen. "May I say that I am elated to see so many new faces. Today's topic is the Ring of Fire. Who can tell me what that is?"

Marty's hand shoots at the ceiling. Mr. Allen ignores it. "Anyone besides Mr. Bellows? Any of our new people?" Mr. Allen then continues to ignore Marty's hand waving around as he tells us that the Ring of Fire is a belt encircling the Pacific Ocean where 80 percent of the world's earthquakes occur. He points to a map of the world and shows how the Ring of Fire matches up with the boundaries of the tectonic plates that cover the earth's surface. Then he passes out a sheet listing all of the disasters we have researched so far. There are several new ones. Amy Chu has written hers in the form of a poem.

## THE BITTER IRONY OF POMPEII
### by Amy Chu
One misty morning in 79 A.D.
Mount Vesuvius erupted in warm Italy.
Spewing volcanic ashes,
Ominous and dark,
Twelve lofty miles into the air they did arc.

Boiling lava raced down the mountain
Faster than a water fountain.
So deeply buried
Were Stabiae and Pompeii
That murals and artifacts were amazingly
        saved!

Two thousand years later, archeologists study
        these towns,
Ancient people captured forever in their every-
        day rounds.
Fetching water, talking to friends,
Or taking a nap.
The destruction preserved them just like
        plastic wrap.

'Tis ironic, to that valley people once more
   have strayed,
Lured by the fertile earth the lava has made.
And still geophysicists
Study Vesuvius
To predict the volcano's next cruel escapade.

## GIANT EARTHQUAKE

When: January 23, 1556
Where: Central China
Details: One of the most deadly earthquakes in history hit Central China and smuched the homes of people. They lived in manmade caves. 830,000 people killed.

## MOST HUMONGOUS EARTHQUAKES IN AMERICAN HISTORY

December 16, 1811–February 7, 1812
Three of the largest earthquakes in American history occurred in the Missouri Territory and were estimated to be 8.8 on the Richter scale (but we can't be sure since the Richter scale wasn't invented until 1935). The first earthquake was so strong it was felt from Quebec, Canada, to Louisiana in the south and as far east as Boston, Massachusetts. In Norfolk, Virginia, the quaking made the church bells ring. One steamboat captain wrote that it made the Mississippi River flow backward!

"Superlative work, folks," says Mr. Allen. "Thanks, Craig Weisener and Marty Bellows for sending in these disasters. Thank you, Amy Chu, for the excellent poem on Pompeii. And thank you, Arlene Welch, for the exceptionally complete report on the Prince William Sound earthquake. Remember, anyone who researches a disaster for our time line gets to go on the all-night field trip."

Now, of course, everyone who came to the first meeting has sent in a natural disaster except me. The bell rings, and Arlene asks me a question as I'm watching Zack walk out with Whitney.

"Huh?"

"I said, why haven't you written up a disaster?"

I look at her and frown. I'm kind of mad Whitney came to this meeting, since she was making fun of it only yesterday. I guess I wouldn't have been mad if Zack had come by himself. And believe it or not, I'm kind of mad Arlene came. This was something I was doing myself, without Arlene to upstage me, and now here she is, and of course she'll be the best as usual. And I'm still mad she rewrote my chapter.

So in a flash of anger, I say, "Because I don't want to, O.K.? Leave me alone."

Arlene's green eyes widen behind her glasses, and I see she is terribly hurt. I put my glasses on my head so that if she starts crying, I can't see it. Then I just take my books and leave.

THAT NIGHT I GET another chapter from Arlene, one she's written by herself. I guess we really are writing separately now, and she is telling about Eva's life (with me adding dialogue), and I'm telling about Lydia's (with Arlene adding description). There's nothing earth-shattering about this. I guess people reading our novel would think that Eva and Lydia are going to get back together again, sometime, at least before the end of the book. But that doesn't have to be true. I print Arlene's chapter and stack the sheets on top of my backpack.

There is one thought in my mind. Even though Whitney made fun of us, I don't care. I still want to go to that dance.

# chapter 16

## Driz, the Rain God

EVA STOOD ON THE rickety stool and propped her elbows on the cold, stone window sill. She closed her eyes and once again, with fierce desperation, tried to send Lydia a message. *Always together, never apart. Your thoughts are my thoughts . . . your heart is my heart.* Three or four times a day, Eva devoted all her energy to sending mental messages to Lydia. She had just about given up on her. There had been no response, except that infuriating color blue, which told Eva nothing except that Lydia couldn't think of anything else except the flying man.

Eva couldn't believe it. After thirteen years of sleeping in the same bedroom, swimming together in the courtyard fountain, making soap minarets of each other's hair in the bathtub, counting the spots on ladybugs, blowing the fuzz off dandelions, and sharing their innermost thoughts, Lydia had forgotten her. Eva was filled with despair.

She opened her eyes. The structure on top of the pyramid had become a beautiful seafaring vessel larger than any Eva had ever seen in Atlantis. Each day she watched as the wooden frame opened toward the heavens like hands cupping a great treasure, its prow arching upward with the grace of a swan's neck. Two tiny men kept up their work, lacing golden reeds tightly from bottom to top with a dogged but lyrical rhythm. People whose homes had been flooded paused with their belongings at the foot of the pyramid on their way to higher ground. Many pointed at the vessel and laughed, but the two workers kept up their pace and paid no attention.

Eva knew who the two men were, even from this distance, because she had watched them for so long. They were the seer Da, slow and purposeful in his movements, and the gentle scribe Talar, who had secretly tutored her and Lydia. Da stopped to rest often, leaning on his cane, but Talar amazed Eva with his capacity for work. From the time he began each morning until the time he stopped at dusk, he barely slowed his pace. Once Talar stood, stretched his back, and wiped his brow, and she thought he looked directly at her. She waved frantically. But he must not have been able to see her. Perhaps she was too high up, or the sun was in his eyes.

Talar, she felt, would help her if he could. He had helped her and Lydia escape from the throne room that day, long ago, when she was a fearless but frivolous princess. In the space of only two weeks of captivity, that life now seemed like a dream. The days had begun to bleed into each other, and now, without any response from Lydia, she had only a thread of hope—that somehow Talar would see her here. Slowly, dully, her mind began to turn over ways to attract his attention.

Suddenly the lock rattled, and the heavy oak door swung open with a rusty squeal so loud, Eva practically tumbled off the stool. She hung onto the window ledge and waited for her eyes to adjust to the dark silhouette in the doorway. Cautiously, she climbed down.

Gradually a slim figure with an imposing headdress and ramrod posture took shape. It was Queen Lannu.

"Hello, Mother," said Eva.

"Eva," said the queen, recoiling, "you look like you haven't bathed in weeks." She wrinkled her nose.

"That's because I haven't."

"Well, I can fix that. We'll get you out of here right

away and into a nice warm bath. And I've brought you a change of clothes." Queen Lannu clapped her hands, and two slaves came in carrying a dazzling tunic sewn with threads of pure gold and orichalcum. Another slave followed; draped over her arm was a heavy necklace laden with precious stones the size of bird eggs. Jewel-encrusted bracelets and earrings dangled from her fingers. In her other hand were sandals that laced all the way up the calf. They were also weighted with precious stones.

"They're lovely, but they're just . . . not me, Mother."

"Have you any idea how much trouble it was to get these things made for you?" cried Queen Lannu. "Look at you. You look like some horrid peasant girl; your hair is a rat's nest. I came to make you a princess again."

"What's the occasion?" Eva asked coldly.

"Why, your wedding. It's all up to you, don't you see? The future of Atlantis is in your hands. Have you seen the people driven from their homes? And still the rains continue. All of the king's advisers agree that our best plan is for you to marry the rain god, Driz."

"What about Lydia? Is she going to marry Driz, too?" Maybe this way she would at least find out where Lydia was.

"I thought it was made clear to you that if you reveal your sister's hiding place and we find her, you will be released until your wedding day."

"I don't know where she is. I swear it." Eva held her head high even though her chin was trembling.

Queen Lannu took a step closer. Eva could smell her mother's musky perfume. She never wore too much or too little, just the right amount. "Then where is the mirror?" asked the queen. "We of course are very anxious to find your sister, but if you tell us the location of the mirror, that may be enough to set you free."

Eva glanced at the slaves, standing at attention, their arms weighed down with the heavy garments. Then she leaned toward her mother as if to impart a spellbinding secret. "I have no idea what you're talking about," she whispered.

"You are a foolish girl," her mother snapped. "I will return in three days. I expect by then you will behave in a civil fashion and be ready for your wedding day." Queen Lannu clapped her hands again, and the slaves left the room, their bare feet soundless on the stone floor. Queen Lannu left the cell and, with a grinding crash, slammed the door behind her.

Eva was suddenly fueled with anger. She had to get out of there. She took the small spoon from her untouched broth and began to dig.

THE THUNDER STONE IN Da's cane had begun to glow so brightly that Talar threw his cloak over it so he could get a few hours of sleep. "Tell me again what the glowing means," he asked as he lay down on a pallet under the long shadow of the ship's prow.

"It means life as we know it will soon be at an end," said Da. "It means a new age approaches."

"That's terrible," said Talar. He wished more than ever that he had never left the farm. Life had become so complicated.

"Only terrible for those who cannot survive in the new age," said Da. "Surely you know by now that you have been chosen to survive, Talar."

Talar stared at the old man's face, then looked up at the star that Da had shown him, the star with the fiery tail that grew each night until now it was almost the size of the moon. He supposed he was glad he had been chosen— except that he believed himself to be a pretty ordinary fellow, and this made him feel a lot of pressure to do something important so that he would really deserve it.

Once Talar had climbed the pyramid, he had never

gone back down. Da had convinced him that returning to his job at the palace was folly. Instead, the old seer had given the scribe a special golden box for storing the tablets and recruited him to help build the ship. Talar didn't know how the shipbuilding supplies had gotten there—he suspected some sorcery on Da's part. But if Da could use magic to get the supplies up here, he wondered, then why not use magic to build the ship, too? But Talar enjoyed the work—it was a nice change from writing all day—and he figured if you're going to have faith in something, you might as well go all the way with it.

"How much longer do we have, wise man?" he asked.

The old seer closed his eyes. "Get a few hours of sleep. We have much work to do and less than a week to do it."

"Who else has been chosen?" Talar thought about his family at home on the farm. And about the bold and fearless young princess, Eva, who had once aimed a ruby-tipped arrow at his heart. He wished he knew where she was. And if she or her sister had been chosen.

"I cannot see the answers to all questions, my son."

Talar turned on his side. Red light from the thunder stone still seeped out beneath the edge of his cloak, and flashes of lightning lit the horizon. Reddish yellow smoke belched from the volcano that loomed in the west. At last he fell into a tired and fitful sleep.

# chapter 17

## The School Dance

ON THURSDAY WHITNEY WAVES at me to sit with her at lunch. I've figured out that if Whitney is getting along with Tracy and Ashley, she's mean to me, but if she's in a fight with them, she's nice to me. They must be fighting today.

"Are you going to the dance tomorrow night?" she asks.

"Are you?" I counter. Zack is sitting with Marty at the next table, and he seems to be looking at us, so I don't glance over. A plan is forming in my mind. "Want to go together?"

"Well . . . ," she says. She looks at her fingernails and tosses her hair over her shoulder. "Maybe."

"My parents said I can't go because I'm still grounded. But maybe I'll just sneak out," I say. "I could ride my bike."

Whitney's almond eyes widen, and she licks her lips with anticipation. She's wearing faint blue eye shadow. "Want me to forge your permission slip? I'm an excellent forger."

"That'd be great. I almost forgot." I dig through my backpack and find the permission slip for the dance. Whitney copies my mom's signature from a volunteer form I have with me. She practices about five times on her napkin, then shows it to me. Beverly Lewis. She has captured my mom's spiky, rushed handwriting pretty well. "How's that?"

"Looks good," I say. I feel a sour taste rush into my mouth when I think about what I'm planning, but I swallow hard. "So, if I ride my bike to your house, can your mom take me?"

Whitney thinks. "Probably," she says.

Friday night I'm supposed to be baby-sitting for Matt while Mom and Dad go to a biology department retirement

131

dinner. I plan to offer him my allowance for a month if he doesn't tell our parents about me leaving. But I luck out because Josh calls and invites Matt to spend the night.

As soon as my parents leave, I change into tight jeans and a spaghetti-strap top Whitney lent me. I slather mousse with a scent called Wild Honeysuckle into my hair, spritz generous amounts of perfume onto any exposed skin, and smear thick coats of shiny, strawberry-flavored gloss onto my lips. I add celery green fingernail polish, blue mascara, and a little silver star glued beside my left eye. I pull my hair back in a kind of messy ponytail with one strand hanging in my eyes on purpose. I can't wear my glasses on top of my head because of the bicycle helmet, but figure I will move them there when I get to the dance.

I slide the house key and a five-dollar bill into my back pocket, straddle my ten-speed, and glide down the driveway, hoping not to see any neighbors. If all goes as planned, I should be back and snug in my bed long before Mom and Dad get home.

I pedal quickly through the neighborhood and the college campus. I pass the gym and then the quad and then the biology building. I pedal as fast as I can, not looking up at Mom's half-moon window as I go by. I pass the turnoff to the pool and Arlene's house.

Every time I think about that chapter she handed me a week ago, with all the changes marked on it, I grit my teeth. I've been mostly sitting by myself during play practice. To top everything off, I've gotten my period again, and it's a lot less exciting the second time around.

I forgot about the fact that I have to ride down Reynolda Road, a busy four-lane, to get to Whitney's house. It's evening rush hour, and people blow their horns at me as they try to get by. I keep my bike as close to the side of the road as I can without falling off the edge. Once, the front wheel slides off onto the gravel, and I barely wrench it back in time. My heart thuds, and my mouth tastes sour again.

It's dark, and by the time I get to Whitney's, it's getting cold. I'm mad at myself for not bringing a sweater. There is no light on her front porch and no car in her driveway. Stepping over the shriveled, potted flowers on her porch, I ring the doorbell. The minutes tick by.

I sit down on the porch steps. Maybe her mom had to run an errand. Maybe they'll be back any minute. For what seems like at least an hour, I sit and wait. I'm freezing.

Maybe Whitney was having a fight with Tracy and Ashley on Thursday but made up after we talked. Finally I admit it— she's not coming. Slowly I stand up and strap my helmet back on, which seems to take forever because my hands are shaking. I wonder briefly if I should just go home, but I'm a little closer to the school. Shaking violently now because I'm so cold, I get back on my bike and pedal out to Reynolda Road.

Cold wind pushes tears across my cheeks. Gusts buffet my bicycle as cars blow by. My breath sears my throat. I finally get to the road that leads to the school and turn off, leaving the roaring rush of traffic behind. When I get to school, I put my bike and helmet behind the Dumpster and lean against the wall of the gym and try, for a long time, to breathe evenly. I finally feel calm enough to walk around to the front of the building.

I see Zack, Marty, and Craig getting out of Marty's dad's Jeep, and I follow a few steps behind. They don't see me. Zack's dark hair is still wet from the shower, and I can see the ridges from his comb. The air is brittle and glittery, and even outside I can feel the vibrations of the music in the soles of my feet. I hand my forged permission slip to Mr. Allen, who happens to be tonight's chaperone.

"How about making a contribution to the natural-disaster time line, Carly?" he says with a smile. He doesn't even glance at the permission slip. "Don't you want to go on the field trip?"

"I don't know." I shrug and smile. Part of me is glad he

cares enough to bug me about it, and part of me wishes he'd leave me alone. "How come you're not wearing your earring?"

He raises his eyebrows and puts his index finger to his lips. "Sh! Have fun now. And, listen, send me an e-mail, pronto."

"I'll try." Inside the air is hot and thick. Strobe lights in blue, red, and orange streak in circular patterns over the gym floor and the ceiling. The music throbs in my temples, in my stomach. It's a sea of sweating, shouting people, and country music is on so loud, it feels as if it's pumping through my veins. The D.J. is Mrs. Boyd, the P.E. teacher, and she loves country music.

I look around, and Zack and Craig Weisener are gone. The only person I know is Marty Bellows. I stand next to him for a minute until I realize that all the girls are standing on one side of the gym and all the boys are standing on the other. I'm on the boys' side.

I sidle under the basketball net to the girls' side. I wonder when Mrs. Boyd will figure out that country music is not our favorite. The gym floor is empty. During slow songs a few people go out and shuffle back and forth with their arms wrapped around each other's waists. Down at the other end of the room, where the girls' side and the boys' side intersect, I spot Zack and Craig standing with Whitney and Tracy and Ashley. I guess Whitney made up with Tracy and Ashley. I look away so it won't seem as if I'm staring—telling myself I shouldn't have expected Whitney to wait for me tonight. When I glance back over, Whitney and Zack are gone.

I walk to the food table so people won't think I'm standing around with no one to talk to or dance with. Miss Norden serves me red punch in a paper cup. She coughs slightly when I lean close, and I wonder if I've put on too much perfume.

"Everything O.K., Carly?" she asks.

"Yeah, fine," I say, faking a big smile.

"Sure?" She raises one eyebrow.

"Sure." I move down the table and pick up a chocolate chip cookie. All of the folding chairs are taken. Someone jostles me, and I spill red punch down the front of Whitney's spaghetti-strap shirt. Unfortunately, when I try to wipe it off, I drag a chocolate chip across it. Oh, man.

I head for the bathroom to wash out the stain. The heavy door to the stairwell is propped open with a wooden wedge. I start through it and notice two people, a few steps below me, sitting on the stairs. I can see their heads, one dark and one blond, inclined toward each other.

It's Zack and Whitney. They're holding hands, their fingers laced tightly together. He's drawn Whitney a superhero cartoon.

"I love it," she says. "Art Woman is me. Cross-Country Man is you."

"I'll make you a new installment every week," he says. Then he adds, "My mom got another promotion. We're moving again right after Christmas."

"Oh no," she says.

"I know." He rubs his shoulder up against hers and sighs.

"Where?" she says after a long minute.

"Boston."

Whitney sits up straighter. "No, it's 'Bahston.'" She says it with a peculiar twangy accent. "Repeat after me: 'Park your car in Harvard yard.'" But she says: Pock ya cah in Ha-vod yod.

He laughs and repeats what she says. I watch the way his eyes move across her face as he leans closer and closer, and they both start to laugh because he's trying to get her to stop talking by kissing her.

Holding my breath, I lean against the heavy door and watch them. I wonder why I've never figured this out, after all the times I've seen them together. I have flash memories of them at the pool that night, at play practice, waiting for our rides on the front steps of the school. Zack likes Whitney, not me. He's never liked me. I feel like the biggest idiot in the world.

I run blindly across the landing into the bathroom and wipe my wet face with a paper towel. The makeup smears, the star migrates from my eye to the corner of my mouth, and my eyes are starting to swell. I try to take deep, even breaths. Blow my nose. Start trying to clean Whitney's shirt, which results in an incredibly huge, muddy-looking stain that seems to get larger every time I rub it.

Outside Mrs. Boyd plays another country song about someone's broken heart. *What about mine?* I want to wail. What does Whitney have that I don't have? We're both wearing spaghetti-strap shirts, tight jeans, strawberry lip gloss, and have our hair in messy ponytails. Why does she look so much better in them? How come she can always think of clever things to say, and I just sit there like a dolt? Why did she desert me tonight? I hate her. I want to be her.

And who am I kidding? I am not descended from mermaid royalty. I am more average than Charlie Brown, and even though my parents are outstanding in every way, there isn't the slightest thing special about me.

I take Whitney's shirt off and scrub it with soap, standing there in the Girls' Room in my bra. Someone comes into the bathroom, but I keep scrubbing without turning around. The stain finally comes out. I climb up on the sink and turn on the hand dryer and hold the soaking-wet shirt under it. At this rate it should be dry by sometime tomorrow.

I'm reaching up to turn the hand dryer on again when suddenly I hear someone crying in one of the stalls.

"Are you O.K.?" I say. "What's wrong?"

"Nothing." The girl comes out of the stall. It's Denise, who plays Sally in *You're a Good Man, Charlie Brown.* She has curly red hair and braces. Her eyes are puffy, and her nose is running.

"Hi," I say. "You're a great Sally."

She stares at me for a minute.

"I'm in the chorus," I say. "Carly Lewis."

"Oh, right. Hi." She splashes water on her face. "Drew just dumped me. Well, actually, he didn't do it himself. He sent J.B. over to do it. I feel like such a loser."

I quickly jump down from the sink. "Don't feel that way. You're not a loser at all. I mean, you got the very best girl's part in the play, and you're great."

She wipes her eyes with a paper towel I hand her. "You sound like my mother. She says we shouldn't waste our time liking guys at this age because they're too immature. She says I should be spending these years of my life on the development of my character."

I run the hand dryer on my shirt again. "I wish I had conversations like that with my mom. All she does is tell me I need to start studying for the SAT and get involved in more extracurricular activities."

"Oh, we talk about that, too," says Denise. "So, did your mom make you be in the play?"

"No, Miss Norden did."

Denise laughs. "Hey, if she cares enough to make you do that, it's a real compliment."

"It is?"

"Sure. It's a great play, isn't it?"

I nod. I realize that my feelings have changed about being in the musical, and it doesn't have anything to do with Zack. I like the songs, the dances, the scenery, the costumes, the clowning around, the excited feeling the whole group gets when everything comes together. And if it wasn't so incredibly scary, I'd even sort of like to have lines by myself.

"Do I look O.K.?" Denise turns around for me.

"You look fine. What about my shirt? Is the stain gone?"

"I can't even tell it was there," she says. "Want to go back out?"

"Sure."

Denise and I find two chairs and talk in between songs. She loves to read and was in a community production of *Annie* last year. In spite of her curly red hair, she didn't get the part of Annie; she was just one of the orphans. She sings me a few bars from "A Hard-Knock Life."

"Give it up, seventh graders!" croons Mrs. Boyd. A pop rock song we all know from the radio starts, and a cheer rises from the crowd. She's finally playing something besides country music. A boy asks Denise to dance. She quickly writes her phone number on my hand and tells me to call her. The dance floor fills. Zack and Whitney are wrapped around each other, barely swaying. I make myself watch them.

A shadow falls over my chair. I glance up, and Marty Bellows is standing in front of me. He has a look of terror on his face, and he sounds like he's hyperventilating.

"So," he says. He checks his watch and presses the button on the side to make it light up. The tiny, neon numbers reflect on his glasses. He looks at me. "Want to dance?"

Hesitantly, I stand up and put my arms around his skinny waist. He holds me like a guitar. We shuffle back and forth on the dance floor.

"You smell good," he says.

WHEN THE DANCE IS over, I walk out with Marty, and he asks me if my parents are coming.

"Yeah, in a few minutes," I say. "I've got to go get something out of my locker."

"Well, then," he says. "See ya." He leans closer. His lips are like a butterfly, shy and fleeting, and they touch mine for only an instant before darting away.

He gets into the Weiseners' van and waves at me through the back window as it pulls away. In a daze, I walk behind the gym and get on my bike. I hardly know what I'm doing. I can't believe that Marty likes me. All this time, I had no idea. Even if I don't know whether I like him back, I guess it makes me feel good that *someone* likes me.

I pedal down Reynolda Road in pitch darkness, teetering as close to the edge of the highway as I dare. Headlights wash over me, casting the speeding shadow of my bike onto the gravel and guardrail beside the road. I am so cold my teeth rattle, and my arms are not just shaking but jerking on the handlebars.

Ever since I saw Zack and Whitney together, I've been turning things over and over in my brain. Zack and Whitney know what it's like to move from one place to another. They know about California and the Big One. Whitney has learned how to reinvent herself again and again with all her new accents and clothes. Zack understands how to slide through a place without really letting it matter whether he belongs. That connects them. Maybe somehow that helps them figure out who they really are. I've been rooted here, in this same place, my whole life. I feel no different from the toddler in my parents' home videos.

I think about something Arlene said once about Shakespeare. That Person A likes Person B, who likes Person C. That's the drama of life. Marty likes me, but I like Zack, who likes Whitney. And I think Whitney is so lucky that he likes her, but to her it seems like no big deal. She didn't even seem that upset when he told her he was moving again, while I feel nearly panicked that he won't be here to watch and daydream about.

I think about what Denise's mother said—that this is the time of your life when you should be working on your character. I feel like one of Mom's blind tadpoles, bumping into the others in the darkness. Maybe one day soon—like them— I will be able to see everything.

Lost in my thoughts, I'm not paying enough attention to the road, and the front wheel of my bike slides off the asphalt. I squeeze the hand brakes and try to jerk the wheel back but can't. The bike skids through gravel and slams into the guardrail. I rocket over the handlebars, land half on the guardrail and half on the ground, and then tumble through shrubs, prickers, and leaves to the bottom of a five-foot drop-off beside the road.

The sky stops spinning. I'm lying on my back. I realize I

am not breathing and draw one shallow and careful breath. There is grass and dirt in my mouth, and I nearly gag trying to spit it out. I try wiggling a toe, a finger, gingerly moving my head. My shin begins to sear with pain, and I think a bug of some sort is crawling on my shinbone. Slowly I sit up and turn my leg so the streetlight above me on the road illuminates it. It's not a bug—it's warm blood running down my leg. There's a huge tear in my jeans.

I take a deep breath and concentrate on not screaming.

"Carly," I say to myself, "this was really dumb." It's comforting to hear my own voice. I have a mental image of bone sticking out through the skin, but my leg just appears to be badly cut and scraped.

My face feels sticky, and I wonder if it's tears or blood. My glasses frames are bent, and one lens has popped out. I take my glasses off with trembling hands and try to bend them back into the proper shape. I don't even attempt the hopeless cause of looking for the lost lens in the dark.

I am really going to get in a lot of trouble. So much trouble. The thought begins to blow up to balloon size and occupy my entire brain.

I scramble up to the road. My leg is throbbing, but I can put weight on it. Dad once told me that means it's not broken. After a couple of cars go by, I climb over the guardrail and examine my bike. The front wheel is totally smashed. I can't even walk it home. Oh, I am going to get in so much trouble.

I sit on the guardrail and look at my mangled bike as hot tears slide down my cheeks. What am I going to do? Think, *think*.

I pull my bike over the rail so it won't get run over and start to limp along the side of the road. My brain churns. Walking to Arlene's would be closer. I picture myself standing on the porch at Arlene's house, and her dad coming to the door. He would let me in. Soft classical music would be playing. Her mother would take me into the bathroom and gently wash my wounds with a washcloth. Both of her parents would know, without any words being spoken, all about my mermaid heritage. That is definitely the place to go. Showing up at home will only get me yelled at.

I walk slowly down the road. The helmet is annoying, so I take it off and thread the chin strap through my belt loop. I watch my looming shadow as a car's headlights sweep by, followed by another car, and another. My leg feels numb, and my jeans are stuck to my leg with blood.

I wonder what my parents would do if they found me dead on the side of the highway. I think about when Tom Sawyer and Huck Finn attended their own funerals, and how surprised they were to hear the nice things said about them. As I limp down the road, I make a list of the people who would say nice things about me at my funeral.

One. Arlene. Then I wonder about that, because she's been getting on my nerves, and I know she has been doubting my inner beauty lately. But I leave her on the list since I am already getting nervous about the list being very short.

Two. Matt. He calls me a dingleberry all the time, true, but surely he loves his big sister.

Three. Keesey. She is not officially a person, and I'm not absolutely sure whether cats can really love people. But she acts affectionate when I'm getting ready to feed her or scratch her head or let her in.

Four. Miss Norden. She thinks I have potential. Maybe I have taken her belief in me for granted. Maybe I really am her pet and just don't know it.

Five. Marty Bellows. He thinks I smell good. Maybe he would say I'm a good kisser, although a person shouldn't be expected to be really good at something the very first time.

Six. My parents. I know that they love me. I just wish . . . I don't know what I wish. Maybe that I was more perfect, like them. Or that they were less perfect, like me.

As I limp along, I think about Whitney. And about Zack. And I don't know about either one of them. I don't know if they would even come to my funeral.

Finally I get to the swimming pool and the cutoff to Arlene's house. But for reasons I don't understand, I decide not to head for Arlene's. I head home.

I've made it all the way to the quad when a car slows behind me. The half-moon window on the top floor of the biology building gazes down like a big, sleepy eye. I stop and turn.

It's a police car. And through the one surviving lens of my glasses, I see Officer Mary Jo Snelling in the driver's seat.

"What seems to be the problem, young lady?"

I'm still sort of crying. I shield my eyes from the headlights, which are shining on my bloody leg and face.

"What's happened to you? Why are you out here by yourself at this hour?"

"I fell off my bike." My voice sounds so strange, like a miniature violin.

She gets out of the car, leaving the door open, and squints at me. "Do I know you?"

"Sort of."

She kneels and shines a heavy-duty flashlight on my leg. "You're going to need stitches here, young lady."

OFFICER SNELLING CALLS MY parents from the emergency room. I am sitting in the waiting room when they run through the automatic doors, still dressed up for the retirement dinner. They are both crying.

I get fifteen stitches in my leg and three above my eyebrow. The helmet pushed my glasses frames into my face when I fell but might have saved my life, the doctor says. My blood is all over Mom's skirt, and she doesn't even care.

ON SATURDAY MORNING IT even hurts to open my eyes. Mom is sitting by my bed with a breakfast tray. "Morning, sweetie. How are you feeling?"

I lick my lips, which are swollen and chapped. "O.K."

"I know we have a lot to talk about, but don't worry about anything now. Just get some rest, and remember that Daddy and I love you very, very much." She kisses my cheek.

As I drift back to sleep, I notice Keesey is curled at the foot of my bed. Mom stops and stares at her. After a few seconds, she scratches her on the head. First Keesey cringes, then she stretches her neck out to allow better coverage.

*Look on the bright side,* I imagine Pollyanna saying. *Your parents still love you. And you're alive.*

*Egyptian princesses can't trust anyone,* says Cleopatra. *My sister tried to poison me.*

*She must deal with the consequences of what she's done,* says Emma.

*Everybody's got to grow up sometime,* says Wendy. *Except Peter, of course.*

Later I notice there is a piece of paper on the breakfast tray. It's another chapter from Arlene. It's less than one page long.

# chapter 18

## Eva in the Tower

EVA SLUMPED UNMOVING ON the floor of her tiny cell, dressed in the heavy jewels and tunic for her wedding to the rain god. She had lost interest in looking out the window. She had completely given up.

She'd tried digging a tunnel with a spoon, but they had found her tunnel and taken the spoon away. She'd attacked the slave who brought her meals, and they had stopped bringing food for two whole days. Now they slid a shallow pan of broth and a crust of dry bread through a slot in the door once a day. The last meal they had given her must have contained some kind of drug because she fell asleep shortly after eating, and when she awoke, she was wearing the wedding clothes. Her other tunic was gone.

She felt weak, and the clothing was heavy. She could hear thunder outside the tower and had actually begun to hope that her marriage to the rain god might help the people of Atlantis somehow. She had seen the columns of people carrying their belongings and moving like a rippling snake up into the hills. She had seen the overflowing rivers and the encroaching tides. She had seen the star the size of the sun, its tail blazing through the sky and growing bigger. Something terrible was about to happen.

# chapter 19

# *The Leonids*

I SPEND MOST OF the day in bed. The leg with the stitches aches dully and feels hot through the bandage. Keesey is sleeping on my desk, on top of the one-page chapter Arlene sent me. Mr. Allen has sent an e-mail, not to all the members of the Young Scientists Club but just to me.

> Dear Ms. Lewis:
> Where is your natural disaster????
> Mr. Allen

My whole life is a natural disaster, I want to tell him. I have no idea what I'm doing or why I'm doing it, and sometimes I feel so mad I could smash everything in my room, and I don't even know why. I feel confused and unlovable, and there is a part of me that is forever lost. For the life of me, I cannot seem to find whatever is supposed to be in its place.

There is one disaster I already know about. I've thought about it so much I don't even have to research it. Sitting on my bed with Keesey curled beside me, I use Dad's laptop to type the legend of Atlantis. I click on Send, and in a nanosecond my e-mail goes to Mr. Allen. I realize with a flicker of sadness that I have used the word *legend,* and that most of me now believes the story of Atlantis is not true. In the same way I've accepted that I live with my true family and am no relation to mermaid royalty, I now believe that the legend of Atlantis was a story Plato made up.

\*      \*      \*

THAT NIGHT MOM AND Dad and I sit on the couch and have a long talk. They tell me they have never been so scared as when they got that call from Officer Mary Jo Snelling. They say that they are very angry I disobeyed them but do not yet know what the right consequences should be. They say I'm lucky to be alive.

I wonder what they are going to do to me. I search their faces. They both look angry, which I expect, but also tired and scared. I decide that I have nothing to lose. I will just tell them how I feel.

"I . . . really wanted to go to the dance. See, there was this guy I liked. But I found out that he doesn't like me. And there was this girl I thought was my friend. But she really wasn't. And . . . I know I haven't been such a good friend to Arlene. But I just wanted to do something on my own." I scrutinize their faces, and to my great surprise, they both look like they might understand. So I plunge on. "I guess I haven't done my best in school so far this year." I glance down at the slightly bloody bandage that hides the even, black stitches on my shin, then breathe and keep talking. "I know colleges are getting more competitive every year. But I'm only twelve, and I'm not ready to take the SAT. I know you guys want me to be perfect like you were, but I'm not." I touch the sore, prickly stitches on my forehead.

"We weren't perfect," they say in unison.

"You make it sound like you were. Winning the science fair and being homecoming queen and valedictorian and on and on."

"I got sent to the principal's office for throwing rocks on the playground in fifth grade," says Dad.

"One of my science projects blew up and destroyed our garage," says Mom. "I was so scared I ran away and hid in the next-door neighbor's barn for a whole day. Our house almost burned down."

I blink, as if blinking will produce entirely new images of my parents. "So why didn't you ever tell me those things?"

Mom and Dad look at me blankly, then at each other. Their faces transform with recognition. Dad takes Mom's hand and smiles at me. "Because we wanted you to think we were perfect."

DAD DRIVES ME TO his office, dark and quiet on a Sunday afternoon. He wants to make sure I didn't injure my eye in the fall, and he thinks he might have a temporary lens that will fit into my bent frames until he can get me a new pair of glasses.

He checks my eye muscles by having me cover one eye at a time and follow his penlight, then uses the biomicroscope to make sure the lids and surfaces of my eyes are O.K. He doesn't talk much, because Dad never talks much, but his hands, when he adjusts my chin, are sure and warm. He sits me in his exam chair and uses the phoroptor, which is a set of rotary lenses that looks like bulky metal goggles floating at the end of a flexible metal arm.

"Look through here," he says quietly, gliding the cold metal device up close to my face. "Which is better . . . one . . . or two?" he asks. The lenses make soft clicks as he rotates through them, searching for the one that will make my vision clearer. The black letters lit up on the wall spring to a new crispness.

"One," I say.

"Good." He clicks through some more lenses. "Which is better . . . one . . . or two?"

I can't tell. The letters on the wall seem the same. I blink, trying to focus my eyes. "Can you do those two again?"

"Sure. One . . . or two?"

"Two."

"Good."

"Dad, is my vision getting worse?"

"Yes," he says, making notes on my chart. "But that's normal. Your vision won't stabilize until you're an adult. It's nothing to worry about."

He pulls away the phoroptor and turns the lights on. Then he takes me into the frame room in the back. Until this year, I loved trying on all the different frames. It was like being in a skit with Arlene, pretending to be someone else.

Now Dad puts on some heavy black frames and says, "Clark Kent here." He takes them off and says, "Also known as Superman." I giggle. He finds a pair of old-fashioned wire rims and holds up one finger, saying, "Nothing in this world is certain but death and taxes."

"Who's that?"

"Benjamin Franklin, the inventor of bifocals."

Giggling, I put on some teeny, round wire rims. "O.K., Dad, who's this?" I try a Liverpool accent. "Give peace a chance, man."

"H'm, that's a tough one," he says. "Mahatma Gandhi?"

"No!"

"Paul McCartney?"

"Paul McCartney doesn't wear glasses!"

"I give up."

"John Lennon!"

"Oh, right. I cannot believe I couldn't figure that out." Dad puts his arm over my shoulder as I try out several different pairs for myself. I look at the two of us in the mirror. Our faces are shaped the same. We have the same eyes and mouth. He has told me jokingly many times that he doesn't know where those ears came from.

"Your mom and I are proud of you," he says. "We're very pleased that you tried out for the play. And we had a long talk last night and agreed that doing well is something you have to want. I wanted to be an eye doctor so badly when I was young that I studied night and day. You can see how much effort your mother puts into her work. She could have focused on being pretty and popular, but she chose academics instead. However, you have to have that dream for yourself. Nobody can live your life for you." He squeezes my shoulder. "Come on, let's go home."

\*     \*     \*

THE NEXT WEEK AT school, Whitney comes up to me and says she's sorry about the dance, that her mom had to work late, and then she got a ride with Tracy and just forgot she said she'd meet me. I can't believe she forgot me, but then I remember that I did exactly the same thing to Arlene a few weeks ago.

I get an empty feeling in my stomach every time I see Whitney with Zack. I avoid Marty because I think I might be embarrassed about kissing him, but I'm not sure. Denise is very friendly at play practice, which is one bright spot. But mostly I feel terrible about Arlene's chapter. Eva is going to be killed if I don't write something to save her.

Mr. Allen sends another e-mail. He has listed my disaster first.

> Hello, Young Scientists!
> And the natural disasters are coming in fast and furious!!! Great work, Carly Lewis, Zack Wingo, Craig Weisener, and Marty Bellows! This field trip is going to be a blast!!!
>
> ### THE LOST CIVILIZATION OF ATLANTIS
> Date: about 1450 B.C.
> One of the hugest disasters of all time was the eruption of the volcano on the island of Thera (its modern name is Santorin) near Greece. Besides the damage caused directly by the volcano, there were earthquakes and tsunamis at the same time, and several other islands were destroyed, including Crete. The Minoans (named after King Minos, the legendary king who kept the Minotaur, or half-bull and half-man) had built civilizations by 3000 B.C. on Crete and Thera that made great advances in art, engineering, and architecture. The Minoans had enormous palaces with courtyards

and baths and colorful painted frescoes. They had a writing system and knew how to make beautiful pottery and jewelry. Some people think the destruction of the advanced Minoan civilization could be the source of the legend about the lost continent of Atlantis.

## TWO-MINUTE BIG ONE
Date: April 18, 1906
An earthquake in San Francisco, California, which lasted only two minutes, demolished most of the city's homes and buildings near the waterfront. Most of the destruction from the earthquake came from fires that started in the city afterward and burned for three days. There have been many earthquakes along the coast of California because of the San Andreas fault, which is a crack in the earth's crust following the coast for about 600 miles. Movement along the fault is about 2.5 inches per year and has added up to almost 200 miles over the last 15 million years.

## TEN-MILLION-TON METEORITE
In 1908 a ten-million-ton meteorite landed in the forests of Siberia and killed reindeer, bears, and wolves in the area. And knocked down trees for 15 miles in all directions.

## MOST HUMONGOUS NOISE EVER MADE
Date: August 26–27, 1883
One of the most famous and humongous volcanic explosions ever was the mountain on Krakatoa, a small island in Indonesia. The noise made during this eruption could be the loudest noise ever made. (If Krakatoa had been located in the middle of the United States, people in all 48 mainland

states could have heard it!) Pieces of dust from the eruption went 50 miles into the sky. As the "cloud" moved around the earth, there were spectacular sunsets and sunrises. This cloud blocked the amount of sunlight reaching the earth and lowered temperatures worldwide for more than a year. Krakatoa's 1883 explosion also produced tsunamis 40 meters high that washed ashore pieces of coral weighing 600 tons. After the explosion two-thirds of the island was gone.

An update on our field trip—we will meet at the school at midnight November 17 and then go to Pilot Mountain to view the Leonid shower, which should reach its peak at about 4 A.M. We will need one or two parent volunteers to drive. Also, you will need a blanket or towel to sit on, and bring warm clothes—it will be cold!! See me for a permission slip at the meeting tomorrow after school. GET PUMPED!
Mr. Allen

THE NEXT DAY AT the meeting of the Young Scientists Club, every seat in the classroom is filled, and people are standing three deep in the back. Mr. Allen can't believe his eyes. In addition to the ten or twelve of us who came to the last meeting, there are at least forty more people. Everyone has scribbled three-line disasters on torn-out sheets of notebook paper.

"We are in dire need of parent chaperones," Mr. Allen says. "And I'm not being facetious."

"WE LUCKED OUT," SAYS Dad. "It's a clear night." He pulls out of the school parking lot and follows the van ahead of him up the highway toward Pilot Mountain. Mom and Dad have volunteered to be chaperones for the field trip, which is comforting and mortifying at the same time. Mom is sitting up front with Dad, and Matt and I are in the center seat. I wanted to make up with Arlene, so I invited her to come with us, but she said she couldn't.

"Hey, kids," Mom says, turning in her seat. "I remember seeing this meteor shower when I was a girl. I was a little younger than you, Matt, and it was when we lived in Arizona. My parents woke me up and took me out in the backyard, and I sat on my dad's shoulders. It was just incredible. The sky was lit up with brilliant shooting stars for more than an hour. I will never forget it."

"So, Mom, was that before or after you burned down the garage?" I wink at Matt, whose eyes practically bug out.

Mom starts to give me a stern look but glances at Dad and laughs. "Uh, I believe that was before the garage-burning incident."

Matt pokes me, whispering, "Mom burned down her garage?"

"Yeah, I'll tell you about it later," I say and squeeze his knee.

"Carly," says Dad, "how often did you say the Leonids peak?"

"Every thirty-three years."

"Next time around," Mom tells us, "you two will be grown up, maybe with children of your own." I try to picture Matt and myself as grownups. I try to imagine what our children will look like. I am pretty sure that by then my brother will have stopped calling me a dingleberry.

The line of cars winds its way up the mountain. When we get out of the van, it's incredibly cold, and the air seems icy and pure as glass. The lights of the city are far away. Everyone is excited, but we're whispering. Mr. Allen gathers us around and talks a little bit about how amazing it is that scientists can predict almost the exact time of the meteor shower. He talks about being safety-conscious on the mountain in the dark. There is a rush of excitement that has an extreme sharpness to it, as if every moment will be etched in memory. We are thrilled by the idea of staying up all night long. We spread our blankets on a small, grassed area next to the summit parking lot. Some people even lie on the asphalt. Mom has brought extra blankets and quilts, and we wrap up in them and lie back to watch the skies.

I think about Atlantis, about Da watching the heavens and tracking the giant comet as it approaches the earth in our novel. I haven't written anything back to Arlene for several weeks. "Hey, Carly," says Matt. "Isn't that Arlene?"

He points to some people on a blanket not too far away. Sure enough, there she is, waving her arms around, telling a funny story or something. She is with Amy Chu and her family.

Mom glances at Arlene. "Why don't you go and say hi?"

I don't answer. This is ridiculous, but I feel betrayed because Arlene is with Amy and not me.

"I invited her, and she said she couldn't come," I say to Mom.

"Go on over and say hi," says Mom. "You're not attached at the hip, sweetie. You're both allowed to have other friends." Grudgingly, I get up and walk over to the blanket where they're sitting.

"Hi, Arlene. Hi, Amy." I stand beside their blanket.

Amy's mom gives me a smile. "Sit down and join us, Carly," she says.

"That's O.K.," I say. "I just came to say hi." Arlene is looking at me. I kneel down beside her. "You told me you couldn't come," I hiss. I know my voice sounds accusing.

"Well, I'd already told Amy I was coming with her," she hisses back. "You think I don't have any other friends besides you. Well, I do."

"What?" I am angry now.

"I know that you don't want to hang around with me anymore. I also know that you and a bunch of your popular friends make fun of me."

"Arlene, I have never made fun of you!"

"You hang out with people who do. What's the difference?"

"They make fun of me, too." I clamp my hands under my arms to warm them. "I thought you didn't know about it."

"I've always known about it." Arlene folds her long legs and wraps her arms around them protectively. She looks away.

"Carly!" Dad calls. "There's a shooting star! It might be starting."

"You better go," says Arlene.

"Just a minute," I call to Dad. I turn back to Arlene. "So you knew that people were making fun of us?"

"Yeah."

I sit down beside her and say again, "I never said anything because I thought you didn't know."

Arlene puts her hair behind her ear. "Well, sometimes it hurts my feelings, and sometimes I don't really care. I mean, I'm going to go away to college and then become a great theater actress, and what these people thought about me in seventh grade won't matter."

Just then I look across the shadowed field, and I see a small, dark silhouette running and leaping. I watch the figure for a moment, and then, even in the dark, from the way he runs, the way he moves, I can tell it's my brother. And in that moment my heart squeezes painfully tight with love for Matt, who is bound to me forever because he is my brother.

And as he collapses onto my parents' blanket, I realize that Arlene is right. She *is* going to become a great theater actress. She believes in herself. She believes that she's special, and that what these kids think really and truly does not matter. "I wish we could still be friends," I say. She doesn't answer me for a minute. A chilly breeze feathers the damp grass.

"I didn't think you wanted to," she says.

I am guiltily silent, then say, "I do now."

"My dad said your writing is . . . pretty good," Arlene adds.

"What?" On the periphery of my vision, the sky begins to sparkle.

"I mean, it's obvious, you blockhead."

The sparkling sky begins to swirl and swim. I blink rapidly.

"Carly!" Mom calls. "Come watch!"

"Just a minute!" I shout. Then, to Arlene, "Truce?" I say.

"O.K.," Arlene says. "But I feel like things can never be the same again."

"Maybe not," I say. "But maybe all friends go through this."

"Yeah," she says. "Maybe."

I stand up and start tiptoeing around the blankets spread on the dark, damp grass. A collective gasp goes up from the huddled, bundled crowd, just like at the Fourth of July fireworks display. I stop and look up. Several long, brilliant flares streak across the sky. There are more cries of delight from the crowd as glowing fireballs etch the sky above my head, then hang for several seconds before they disappear.

For some reason I feel like skipping. And so I do, all the way to our blanket. With each skip I am flying, for a second or so, in the glassy air. And I slide under the quilt Mom has spread over our family. For an hour we lie there and look up, dazzled. Dad's arm is around Mom, and Matt and I are curled on either side of them. We snuggle close to feel their warmth.

I watch the meteors flash and fade. Each one blazes a trail for only an instant and then is gone. On a blanket nearby are Arlene and Amy, and somewhere there is another blanket, where Zack and Whitney are probably snuggling. Out of the corner of my eye, I see a tiny, lonesome green light flashing on and off once in a while. That's probably Marty's watch. Next time this meteor shower peaks, thirty-three years from now, Arlene might be a famous actress, and maybe Marty will be a doctor or a musician. And maybe Zack and Whitney will have moved five or six more times and forgotten all about each other. And I don't know where I will be, only I will be grown up and maybe I will be a writer and maybe married to someone I won't even meet for ten or fifteen more years, and the people who seemed so important in middle school will have faded in my memory the same way the meteors, which are only tiny pieces of dust, extinguish in the sky.

And I think of all the natural disasters that have happened to humankind, all of the earthquakes, and tsunamis, and volcanic eruptions, and hurricanes, and droughts, and plagues, and collisions with meteors. And we're still here. We've survived. If people can live through all they've lived through, well then surely I can survive my own life. I feel a spreading sense of peace in my chest.

"Imagine what it must have been like for those people back in 1833, when they thought the sky was falling," says Mom.

"The most amazing thing about this meteor shower," Dad says, "is that the bits of space dust passing through our atmosphere and lighting up tonight's sky were shed by the comet Tempel-Tuttle sometime around 1766."

"Whoa," says Matt. "Now that is freaky."

BACK HOME, IT'S PAST six in the morning and I am so sleepy, but I've finally decided how to answer Arlene's one-page chapter. I type two pages and click Send.

Now that I have written the chapter, my mind unwinds into a dream about Eva and Lydia, hiding together in the banyan tree. Through the sounds of the wind feathering the leaves of the mighty oak outside my window, I slide into sleep.

# chapter 20

## *Lydia Decides*

"TODAY IS THE DAY. I can feel it," Leorbur said as he began to attach the silken balloon to the basket Lydia had helped him construct. He had built a roaring fire nearby with a complicated funnel system for feeding the hot smoke into the mouth of the balloon. "Our dream of flying is about to come true."

"Well, actually—" Lydia tied a hemp line from the basket to the edge of the balloon. Leorbur had not kissed her again since the first time. It had been very special, that kiss, her heart trapped like a moth inside her chest, but face it, that kiss had only lasted about three seconds out of her entire life, which was nearly thirteen years. And somehow the kiss was less special because she couldn't tell Eva about it. Lydia found herself wishing she could talk to Eva about everything.

In the past few days messages from Eva had become more frequent. HELP, I'M IN THE TOWER. Lydia had again mentioned them to Leorbur, and again he said he must get the balloon aloft first. Yesterday afternoon, the same time the storms started, the messages had suddenly stopped.

Now a whole day had gone by without a message. It suddenly occurred to Lydia that Eva might be dead. Abruptly, she stood up from her work and stared back over the flooded valley toward the palace. Black spots floated across her vision.

Leorbur attached the last hemp line and stretched the balloon out along the ground, and then fit the funnel from the fire into place.

"Here goes!" Leorbur cried. The huge, silk balloon began to puff and writhe like a live thing as the hot air spilled inside. Nya, tethered nearby, stamped her feet and tried to back away. Leorbur's face split wide in a crazy, joyful grin. "It's working!" He whirled across the clearing, grabbed Lydia's shoulders, and kissed her. Cupping her face in his hands, he kissed her again.

As the balloon grew, so did the towers of black clouds on the horizon. Thunder rumbled and growled. The ground trembled, and dense smoke poured from the volcano. Lydia saw a flash of lightning. Nya snorted with alarm and tossed her white mane. It looked yellow in the strange light.

"Leorbur, this might not be the best time—"

"Get in, get in!" he shouted. The balloon was filling rapidly, and the reed basket began to slide along the ground. "Now!" He climbed into the basket and grabbed Lydia's wrist. "It's the storm, Lydia; it's my dream. This is it. Get in!"

"What about Nya?" Lydia couldn't believe she hadn't thought about Nya until this moment. The balloon would never carry a horse.

"You have to leave her. Come on!" Leorbur's eyes were an electric blue, and his golden ringlets trembled. He clasped Lydia's hand so tightly, it hurt. The balloon billowed and reared into the sky.

And suddenly Lydia yanked her wrist free. "No!"

The wind dragged the basket and Leorbur several feet away. He reached out to her. Thunder clapped, and a few sloppy raindrops fell. And then the balloon began to rise, taking Leorbur with it. He looked down at her with anguish. "Lydia!"

Lydia stood her ground and watched the balloon clear the treetops. Nya whinnied again, and Lydia ran to her, swiping her cheek with the back of her hand to erase the tears.

# chapter 21

# Curtain Call

I AM SITTING AT the desk in Arlene's third-floor bedroom with the stars on the ceiling. One leg is tucked underneath me. Arlene is lying on her bed, doing her scissors exercise. The nub imprints from the bedspread are on the backs of her long, skinny legs. She is dictating the end of the story of Atlantis, and I'm typing. What I type is not exactly word for word what she says. In fact, I make a lot of changes.

One floor down Juliet is listening to rock music, and one floor below that Mrs. Welch's string trio is practicing a classical piece by Puccini. Tonight after dinner Arlene and I are going to act out *My Fair Lady* for her parents. I'm going to be Eliza Doolittle, and Arlene will play all the other parts.

Things are O.K. between Arlene and me. After our talk during the Leonids, and after I wrote the chapter where Lydia leaves Leorbur to try to save Eva, she and I started sitting together again at play practice. We didn't talk too much about what had happened. I think she's right that things will never be the same again. But they're O.K. for now.

Last weekend the play went great. For about the first thirty seconds after I walked onstage, I saw the faces floating out there in the dark, and there was roaring in my head, and I nearly pitched forward right on my face, but eventually my senses settled down. I was close to being on key and only forgot one line. I did the first act without my glasses but on my last exit tripped over someone's foot, and Miss Norden suggested that no one would care if I wore glasses for the second act, so I did. I really like the new ones Dad got me, anyway.

Zack was great as Schroeder, and Arlene was a terrific Lucy. The scene where Arlene chased Zack around the stage trying to kiss him was the funniest in the whole play. I stood in the wings and watched the scene, and later was standing at stage right waiting to go on for the curtain call when I saw Zack kiss Whitney backstage. Whitney walked right up to him, and he put his hand on the back of her head and pulled her toward him until her lips met his. I looked away. It was ironic (that was a word in Miss Norden's class this year) how I liked Zack so much, and he kissed Arlene onstage, and Whitney backstage, but never kissed me. It still bothers me a little, but I keep telling myself that sometimes you just have to accept stuff that happens in life.

And guess who got the longest standing ovation and who all of a sudden I realized might even be famous when he grows up? Marty. When he came out, his glasses glinting under the single spotlight, and sang "Suppertime," something amazing happened. He was no longer a jittery and weird little guy but someone completely different, a kid with a smooth and soaring voice who, if only for that moment, knew who he was and where he was going. I saw his parents in the audience, and they both looked perfect, so well dressed with every hair in place. They looked strict, and I wondered what would happen if Marty decided he wanted to become a musician instead of going to medical school. I'm glad my parents are trying to accept me for who I am, and I told them I'll let them know who that is as soon as I figure it out.

We gave Miss Norden an armful of roses afterward, and she got so choked up, she had to pull a tissue out of her sleeve and blow her nose. "This is a great bunch of kids," she said. I think whatever it was Miss Norden wanted from us, we gave it to her when we put on the play.

She came up to me after the curtain call and said, "Well, Carly, are you going to audition for the next one?"

And I said, "Yeah, I think so. Thanks for making me do it."

"My pleasure, Carly," she said. She smiled, and the lines on her forehead went away.

"Miss Norden?"

"Yes?"

"When you were my age . . . were you ever mixed up about stuff?"

She blinked rapidly and cleared her throat. "All the time," she said. "You remind me a lot of myself when I was your age." She squeezed my shoulder. "I'm going to be on your case again in the spring when it comes time for the literary festival. I expect you to enter." Someone came up to ask her something, and she whisked away.

Mom and Dad gave me a beautiful bouquet of daisies, and Mom took my face in her hands and said, "Carly, we are so proud of you." Dad hugged me and said I was his favorite member of the chorus. Matt didn't call me a dingleberry for the whole night.

Arlene's parents sat with mine. Arlene's father pronounced the production to be "splendid, simply splendid." And then, I was so amazed, he pushed his glasses up on his nose just like Arlene and said to me, "I've enjoyed reading the novel you and Arlene are working on, Carly. You're a fine writer. Keep it up."

Josh and his mom were sitting right behind my parents, and Mrs. Greenberg smiled at me. I tried to figure out which eye was the false one, but both of her eyes were a lovely shade of sky blue, and they looked exactly alike.

Mr. Allen came to the play, and I saw him talking to Marty. He gave me the thumbs-up sign as he was leaving, and I saw a gleam in the center of his earlobe. He was wearing his earring.

"You were fabulous," I told Marty. "Nobody could have played Snoopy better than you."

"Hey, thanks." He turned beet red and pressed the button that lit up his watch. "Hey, the next Young Scientists field trip is to check out the Raleigh planetarium. You have to add another disaster to the time line to go. You going?"

"Yeah," I said. "I can come up with another disaster, no problem."

Now that I've done the play, I would tell anybody that if you're really, really scared to do something, then you should just try it, because even if you don't do a fabulous job, even if you just do an O.K. job, what counts is that you tried in spite of the fear.

"GOT IT SO FAR?" Arlene says. She's trying a yoga position where you sit cross-legged and lean forward and touch your nose to the floor.

"Yeah." I finish a sentence and punch in the period with a flourish.

"You know, now that we're getting close to the end . . . I don't want anybody to die," Arlene says. "I like all our characters."

"Me, too, but let's be realistic, Arlene. A comet hits the earth. There are earthquakes and a volcano and a hundred-foot tidal wave."

Arlene gets up and stands, arms akimbo, in front of her bookcase. "*Actually*, somebody dies in all really good books, don't they?"

"Well, let's think . . . *Charlotte's Web.*"

"I cried for two whole days," she wails, throwing her long arms in the air.

"Me, too." My eyes sting, just thinking about Wilbur with that mouthful of spider eggs, and how Charlotte was both a true friend and a good writer.

"And there was Aslan in *The Lion, the Witch and the Wardrobe,*" she adds.

"Oh, and Beth in *Little Women*—" I groan. "And what about *Bridge to Terabithia,* when—"

"Don't even talk about it. It's just unutterably sad."

"Unutterably? Is that a word?"

"Of course." Arlene sits on her bed and takes off her glasses and wipes her eyes. I do the same. Arlene puts her glasses back on. I do the same. We both sigh, long and drawn out, as if our sighs carry the woes of the world. There is a long moment of silence.

"Oh." I snap my fingers. "In *Peter Pan* Tinker Bell *almost* dies, but she comes back to life if the audience claps hard enough."

I look across this room that I love, with the slanting floor and the stars on the ceiling, at my friend and fellow writer. I have to admit, I've done some pretty stupid things so far this year. I think about the swimming pool fiasco, about the bike accident, about the fights with my parents, about all the hurt feelings, about what a terrible friend I've been.

But I am proud of some of the things I've done. Being in the play. My new relationship with my parents, where we actually talk about things. And I finally stood up for Arlene. The last week of play practice, after Arlene's mom had picked her up, Whitney was starting to imitate her, waving her arms around, walking knock-kneed, and saying, "Well, *actually,* the arthritic phenomenon of catastrophic wavelengths in Shakespeare's day was infantile—" and I heard myself saying, "Whitney, stop being so mean. Arlene is my friend. I know that you can be a nice person if you want to." It was great because Whitney could not think of a single comeback.

So now Arlene and I are about to finish our novel. I want to make the last chapter really good because who knows whether Arlene and I will write any more books together. She said she's going to be pretty busy practicing to take the SAT. Also, she's been writing poetry on Friday nights with Amy, and I've been doing stuff with Denise. I might like to try writing something by myself, maybe a play, for the spring literary festival. One thing I've learned—for a story to be good, it has to have both love and a quest.

"Earth to Carly," Arlene is saying. "Do you think somebody has to die at the end of our book?"

"I don't know," I say. "Let's just write the last chapter and see what happens."

# chapter 22

## *The Meteor*

TALAR FINISHED THE HISTORY of Atlantis and wrapped the clay tablets in a wax-soaked goatskin for waterproofing. Then he placed them inside the box made of polished gold that Da had given him. He closed the tightfitting lid and placed the box in a special protected compartment in the prow of the completed vessel. As Da had instructed, he had gone into town and bartered for several dozen bags of dried fruit and grain, as well as a rooster and two hens in a cage. He had filled one hundred ceramic jars with fresh water. Everything was ready.

The thunder stone on the head of Da's cane pulsed with a light so bright, it could be seen from a mile away, even during the day. Purple clouds were stacked on the horizon, lit from behind by flashes of lightning, and the sky was a strange color of orange-yellow. The star with the enormous tail arched across the sky.

NYA KNEW THE WAY home. Lydia leaned against her neck and let the mare have her head. She worried briefly about the fire Leorbur had left blazing on top of the ridge but decided that the rains would put it out. Nya settled into a tireless gallop.

They were able to skirt several flooded valleys, and Lydia was shocked to see only the top branches of the banyan tree in the last of them. She remembered hiding there behind the sheltering leaves the first day she and Eva had run away.

The rocky river shallows on the edge of the palace grounds had become a roiling, white-capped rush of water three times as wide as before. Lydia pulled back on Nya's reins in panic, but the mare plunged in without hesitation. When Nya lost her footing and began to swim, Lydia simply hung on, the icy water numbing her legs.

The mare's breathing was high-pitched and heavy as she swam, and Lydia whispered encouragement, her lips brushing a smooth, silver ear. The current pushed them a hundred yards down the river before Nya was able to regain her footing. Just past the royal vineyards and the palace stood the tower.

"Come on, girl. We're almost there."

The royal vines hung heavy with untouched grapes past their peak for harvesting. Eddies of muddy water swirled in the palace courtyards. Nya slowed to a walk, and Lydia gaped at the unused furnishings and empty rooms. In the royal dining room the hundred-foot-long eucalyptus table was still spread with dishes spilling with lamb shanks, grapes, figs, bread, and wine. But not one person was there. She passed the window to her own bedroom and saw a lovely tunic and jewels lying on the bed as if a slave had carefully laid them out just this morning for her. A chill went up her spine.

Poseidon's temple was deserted. The water in the fountains lay stagnant, and the gold and copper statues had dulled to a gray-green. Lydia urged Nya up a narrow path behind the temple leading to the tower. At the foot of the stone steps that spiraled to the tower's peak stood a group of horses, some with riders. Nya tossed her head, and Lydia saw that one of the horses was Sphinx. Sphinx was tethered, riderless.

"Easy, girl, easy," Lydia murmured to Nya. As she approached, Lydia recognized the riders as her mother, her father, several soldiers, and the three seers, all in ceremonial dress.

Suddenly she had an idea. If only she had time! Before anyone saw her, she whirled on Nya, raced back to the palace, and galloped into the courtyard outside her own bedroom. She climbed through the window and grabbed the jeweled tunic, then stood uncertainly for a moment, glancing one last time at the things that had surrounded her as a child. Then she ripped down the filmy mosquito netting covering the bed and vaulted out the window.

EVA HEARD CRIES AND hoofbeats outside the tower window. She lifted her head.

"Eva's escaped! After her!"

Dreamlike, she got to her feet and climbed onto the stool. Outside the window the sky was lit by a massive star whose enormous tail arched across the heavens, casting an eerie brightness even though it was close to sunset. Eva rubbed her aching eyes.

Down below a silver horse streaked by with a figure on its back. The rider wore a gorgeous tunic, identical to the one Eva had on. As the horse passed by Sphinx, the black mare reared and neighed, and then with a mighty jerk of her head, she yanked her tether loose and thundered after.

Nya! And Lydia!

The soldiers, the seers, and the king and queen all urged their mounts down the path after the runaway horses. With a weak smile, Eva watched the distance lengthen between the horses and their pursuers.

"Run, Sphinx. Run, Nya," she whispered. And then, far in the distance, she saw something amazing—an enormous balloon with a basket attached skidding through the air just below the banks of clouds. The light from the star's tail glinted on the rider's blond curls. The flying man— finally flying!

She thrust her arm between the bars of the window and waved frantically. "Help!"

Then she heard footsteps on the stones outside her cell. One of the guards must not have followed the horses. Eva jumped down and crouched behind the door, the stool poised above her head.

The deadbolt rasped, and the heavy door squealed. Eva jumped up and swung the stool as hard as she could.

Someone moaned and thudded to the floor. It was Lydia. With a gasp, Eva knelt and grasped her sister's hand. "Oh no, what have I done?" A greenish black welt was rising on Lydia's forehead. "Always together, never apart," whispered Eva. "Your thoughts are my thoughts . . . your heart is my heart." Lydia's tunic, Eva noticed, was nearly in threads, but she was brown and muscled from her work outdoors. Eva was pale from her captivity in the tower. They looked very different now.

One of Lydia's eyelids twitched. She brought her hand to her forehead and winced.

"Lydia, are you all right? Thank Poseidon you're awake. I'm so sorry." Eva helped Lydia to a sitting position and pulled her close. "I was afraid I'd never see you again."

Lydia wrapped her arms around her sister's thin neck and hugged her, nearly choking with relief and guilt. "Please don't be mad at me. I was getting your messages for days and ignoring them because I didn't want to leave Leorbur."

"You got my messages? It worked. Our mind reading worked!" Eva grinned, then thought a moment. "Wait a minute." She met Lydia's eyes. "Let me get this straight. You were getting my messages . . . but you were ignoring them."

"I'm sorry, Eva. I am so sorry."

Eva glanced at the stool. "Maybe I'll hit you again."

"I wasn't much of a sister—but there was something I needed to find out."

"Well, you came. That's what counts." The sisters held each other tightly for a long moment. Suddenly Eva remembered something. "Lydia, do you still have that mirror?"

"Yes." Lydia pulled the mirror from her pocket. They looked at its surface and saw two faces, one pale and one tanned, looking back. "We're both there now. How strange."

"There's something magic about that mirror. We have to keep it."

A thunderclap split the sky, and Lydia jumped, dropping the mirror. In one blinding second, it broke in two. Lydia scooped up the pieces and thrust one in Eva's pocket, the other in her own.

Eva suddenly leaped to her feet, pulling Lydia up with her. "I almost forgot! Leorbur—he's coming in his balloon!"

They both ran out onto the landing at the top of the stone steps. Leorbur's balloon was only five stadia away, about to sweep by in the ferocious winds. Several soldiers on horseback streaked up the path toward the tower.

"By Poseidon's beard, look!" Eva pointed.

"I guess they figured out it wasn't me riding Nya," Lydia said.

"I meant to ask, who was that in the wedding tunic?"

"A wadded-up mosquito net."

Eva laughed. "Good one!"

"Catch!" Leorbur's voice was nearly lost in the wind. He heaved a hemp rope at them as his basket swung by. Lydia and Eva glanced at each other, terror in their eyes, then snagged it and leaped out. They both screamed as the valley yawned far beneath their swinging feet. The horsemen stopped and looked up at the balloon and its dangling cargo, then followed it, ready to capture anyone who fell.

"Climb, Lydia! Climb, Eva!" Leorbur leaned over the edge of the basket, hauling the line up bit by bit.

The girls dangled, buffeted by the gale, the rope searing their palms. Lydia started to shinny up monkey-style.

"I'm slipping!" Eva shouted from below. Her tunic and jewelry were weighing her down.

"Hold on!" Leorbur shouted.

"I'll climb up and help Leorbur pull you in! Don't let go!" Lydia was glad now that she'd built her muscles helping Leorbur weave the basket for the balloon.

"HOIST THE SAILS!" SHOUTED Da, thrusting his glowing cane above his head. Da's beard flapped like a tattered flag in the ripping wind.

As far as Talar could see, this boat was high and dry on top of the pyramid and not likely to sail anywhere anytime soon. Sure, it was raining, and a lot of low-lying areas of Atlantis were flooded, but it was still going to have to rain a heck of a lot for the water to get up here. Besides that, Atlanteans had always been taught not to sail in a storm.

Still, Talar had faith in Da and did as he was told. Hand over hand, he hauled on the halyard, and the mainsail raced up the mast, billowing and thrashing in the wind.

THE METEOR PLUNGED TOWARD the earth. It smashed into the atmosphere and became a boiling fireball streaking toward the ocean. With an explosion of golden light, it slammed into the sea, carving a wave one hundred feet high that hurtled toward Atlantis.

EVA'S HANDS WERE SLIPPING. Her palms burned. She gritted her teeth and squeezed her eyes shut, but she could not hold on any longer. Lydia and Leorbur, safe in the basket, heaving the rope over the edge, cried out to her not to give up. Only ten feet more.

The storm pushed the balloon west of the city toward the pyramid, leaving the royal horsemen far behind. Only nine feet more.

The wind rose to gale force. Eva could not hold on any longer. She heard Lydia scream, "Eva, no!" She tried to call out to Lydia but couldn't. She felt a sensation of cool whiteness. And then she fell.

AT FIRST TALAR THOUGHT a large bird, such as an albatross, had somehow blundered into the mainsail. He was still seeing black spots from the enormous explosion out in the ocean a few minutes before. He was sweating profusely, and time seemed to be moving slowly, and he thought he might be capable of nearly anything, of lifting the pyramid in his bare hands if need be.

Then he saw strange visions—a giant balloon racing west, and two horses, a black one and a silver one, galloping up the steps to the pyramid and up the ramp onto the vessel.

"Ho, easy, there." Talar thought the horses might be part of a dream, but they sidled into each other and showed him the whites of their eyes, so he tried to soothe them. The black bore an empty golden saddle while the silver mare had a jeweled tunic strapped to her saddle. The tunic was strangely stuffed with mosquito netting. Talar didn't think Da had planned on taking horses along. They would certainly eat a lot of grain. But he led them down the ramp to the storage and sleeping compartments below the deck. He forgot all about the bird until Da called to him from the other side of the mainsail.

"Talar, come here. Help me."

Talar climbed to the upper deck, battling ferocious winds and rain. And he saw that what had fallen into the mainsail wasn't a bird but a pale princess dressed in a tunic laden with gold and jewels.

"Princess Eva!" he cried.

"She is still breathing," said Da. "Help me take her below. Quickly."

Talar lifted her by himself. She weighed very little. If it weren't for the jewels and precious metals in her garments, she might weigh nothing at all. Da touched her blistered fingers with the thunder stone on his cane, and they were healed. He went ahead of Talar down the ramp to arrange a pallet for Eva to lie on.

Before Talar carried Eva below, the sky grew suddenly dark. He glanced at the eastern horizon. Something huge and black had risen out of the ocean and totally blocked out the sun.

THE HUNDRED-FOOT TIDAL wave hit Atlantis at a speed of five thousand stadia per hour. The impact of the meteor caused earthquakes and dislodged a humongous rock blocking the mouth of the volcano. The volcano erupted in a towering jet of blistering magma, and the entire island was destroyed in one night.

Leorbur, the flying man, and Lydia glided west ahead of the storm winds until morning, when the balloon gradually sank lower in the air until it touched down and bobbed on the surface of the Atlantic. Leorbur and Lydia floated for two weeks, drinking rainwater and eating fish they caught by dragging the balloon, until they landed on what may or may not have been an island in the Caribbean Sea.

The tidal wave engulfed the pyramid with stupendous force, lifting the vessel built by Da and Talar off the peak, and it raced west with the waves. As the tides receded, however, the vessel circled back with the ocean currents due east and maintained that course for two months, after which time Da, Talar, Eva, and the horses had consumed most of the food and water. They had nearly given up when they sighted the shore of what may or may not have been Africa.

Da lived to be over a thousand years old, and all the children called him Grandfather and revered his wisdom. Talar had a life in the country once again, where he made many copies of the history of Atlantis and told it to everyone he met. Even those who did not believe it was true thought it made a good story.

Leorbur never stopped trying to find better ways to fly and, in time, invented several sets of colorful wings so that the young princes and princesses could glide from their mountain palaces down to the black sand beaches without burning their feet.

Eva and Lydia both became strong, wise queens who governed with fairness and love. Whenever they looked into the broken halves of the Mirror of the Oracle, they saw each other, and they frequently sent mental messages winging their way across half a planet at more than the speed of light.

> *Always together,*
> *never apart.*
> *Your thoughts are my thoughts . . .*
> *your heart is my heart.*

# acknowLedgments

HEARTFELT THANKS GO, ONCE again, to my dear writing family—Maggie Allen, Jean Beatty, Ann Campanella, Ruth Ann Grissom, Nancy Lammers, Carolyn Noell, and Judy Stacy—for listening to poor Carly's troubles for over a year.

Fred Leebron is an extraordinary writing teacher, without whose support and encouragement I probably would not have gotten beyond the first twenty pages.

I will always treasure Debby Vetter's unbridled enthusiasm (sorry about the pun, I couldn't resist) for this book. In so many ways, she understood what I was trying to write better than I did. She has expertly and sensitively helped me shape this book.

Two writing partners from my youth—Pepper Potter and Jan Hausrath—helped inspire this story. Some of the thrilling adventures we wrote are still boxed in my closet at my parents' house. (Don't worry, that's exactly where they will stay!)

I'd also like to thank Dr. Barbara Lom, a biology professor at Davidson College, for showing me her lab and research techniques and for reviewing the lab scenes. When my first novel, *Eleanor Hill,* won the North Carolina Award for Juvenile Literature, I attended an American Association of University Women conference to make a presentation. Also making a presentation was Dr. Lom, whose research on the development of retinal neurons in tadpoles had been awarded an AAUW grant. Dr. Lom's description of her work was totally captivating. I was fascinated by the concept that a developing tadpole can be blind one night and by the next morning able to see.

I would also like to thank Dr. Steven Friedman for taking his time to talk with me about optometry and for reviewing the scenes that took place in the optometrist's office.

Although I created the book's time line using half a dozen time lines from various reference books, the natural-disasters time line on the Tar Heel Junior Historian Association Web site gave me the first inspiration to create such a time line for Mr. Allen's science club.

Ms. Amy Becton takes care of Earl, the skeleton who hangs out in the lobby of the Davidson College biology building, and I appreciate her assistance. Last but not least, I would like to thank Earl himself, for the naked honesty that transcends his extensive wardrobe and for his unflinching willingness to make a cameo appearance in *The Princesses of Atlantis.*